3

Chapter 1

Doyle's Farm, Cambletown: September 8th 1924

The Awakening

Owen lay asleep, it was an uneasy sleep, a black sleep and a torment of questions festered in his mind. He teetered on the brink; untethered he slipped and lingered in uncertain dreams and shadowed valleys, as he waited for the dawn light to splinter the darkness of his memories. He was sleeping in his mother's old bed, the one he was conceived in, suckled and weaned in and the one his father died in. It was a bed stained in memories and forgotten dreams. Outside it was raining and the blustery wind rattling on windows swelled the night's uneasiness as he tossed to and fro like a tide surging and surging across the Galtee sands. He stirred, as the soft caress of his mother's hand washed across his eyes and face. Like the tide he calmed and stirred, calmed and stirred. It was warm and gentle and yet, and yet it beckoned him to wake. Half-waking, half-craving sleep he stirred again, his eyes flickered open, not recognising the shapes and shadows of the room. "Owen! Owen! " his mother's voice in a strong Irish brogue pressed quietly but forcefully through the cold night air. Lightning flashed across the mirror and faces on the landing and sensing danger Owen woke with a start. "Muther?" He instinctively held her outstretched hands. A ripple of movement ran through the figures on the landing as they muttered and waited, and shifted awkwardly from one foot to the other. They had entered the house in stealth and secrecy, craving refuge within its walls, and now were vigilant in their surveillance, less they be discovered.

"Owen. Listen." With the dreams still fixed on his retina he lifted his head with a wide-eyed and questioning look as if he had woken in some unremittingly dark, Stygian underworld. She stroked the thick black hair from his eyes and setting her hands on his shoulders she raised him up from the yellow and sweat covered pillow. She was highly agitated and fidgeted unnecessarily with the blanket covers. Her lips quivered before she spoke. "I want you to go for the Doctor, Doctor Lewis," she corrected herself unknowingly, " he's in Kilshanny village tonight. Matt is worse, it's not good". She tightened her lips and swallowed hard, as if trying to stem the rising wave of emotion in her body. The unsteady flame, of a small, blackened, brass oil lamp on the bedside table, seemed to brighten and flicker in the cold stream of air flowing through the open bedroom door. Owen nodded as his eyes glanced across the hallway at the on-looking faces peering through the dimly-lit shadows. He tried to take in the faces around without arousing interest. He glanced again but did not hold his gaze for long. He had learnt this from his father. The priest moving silkily from man to man, touching hands; the solicitor from mid-town occasionally whispering in his mother's ear, she laughed uneasily; the chandler still wearing an apron standing uncomfortably alone; two of O'Leary's farm hands, both unshaven, at the back of the landing, nervously wandering back and forth, to the window that overlooks the front yard and Connor. "Muther what's going on?"

"No time Owen, we'll talk later," little knowing that this would be their last conversation for some time. Owen acknowledged the priest, stood in the doorway that was part of four connected rooms running north to south across the house. He glimpsed the two half -hidden shadowy figures behind him, both carrying guns. They stood like the Archangels of death. The smaller one rubbed the holster and butt of the gun as if expecting unwanted company. Owen instinctively knew they were from the Brotherhood. Extreme Republicans from out of the County could only mean trouble he thought. Sinn Fein had found its voice with De Valera made President, having established a political platform broad enough to hold all Irish men who believed in independence. But was it the Ireland that was dreamed of? He knew his father had taken part in many meetings with these oath-bound fanatical individuals set on the creation of an independent, democratic Republic of Ireland by force if necessary. But none to his knowledge had ever set foot in the house before. But didn't his father want, didn't he want, didn't we all want a free Ireland? Owen knew from birth that the true Irish were Gaelic and Catholic. It had been drummed into him. But he also knew much of Ireland had been shaped by migration and invasion. Whether he liked it or not, the Irish people had been fucked by most Europeans across the centuries. Catholics and Protestants alike as Liam used to say. He always remembered his father's words, "Was Carson, a Protestant Leader, any less of a patriot because he wanted union with the British than any other true Irish man? Was De Valera a patriot merely because he smuggled arms using his own private yacht." With Michael Collins dead at thirty- one, killed by his own countrymen, and people wondering what part De Valera played in his assassination, the mood of Ireland was changing. But would change be possible without all the killing? Would more good people die in vain? His eyes flashed across the partially exposed tattooed words of "L'Eireann" on a bare forearm. He was shocked to see Father Ryan. Was Matt that far gone? Was poor Matt dying? For a few minutes Owen listened intently to the murmuring voices and studied some of the familiar faces in the room. He watched the muted, under the breath comments realising this was a meeting of great importance. Was this a gathering of the local bad boys? Ireland was rising and the drive to be one was reaching the killing point. The Brotherhood had staged the Easter Rising some eight years ago, but after the executions everyone in Ireland knew, except the fucken British, that the Republicans could no longer settle merely for Home Rule. The killing of the fourteen Irish protesters at Croke Park and the assassination of the Lord Mayor of Cork City had seen to that. Croke Park was now sacred ground and it would be a long time before God Save the King would be sung again in its hallowed terraces. The stakes had been raised. Treaty or no treaty, Ulster was the prize and the battle-ground, the fourth green field. The killing of Irish and British would go on. It did not matter it was now a different war. Out of the muttered tones the occasional angry word filtered through. "Tell fucken O'Leary to get rid of the delivery. Tell him he needs to clean the Mausers up, grease them off before he conceals them."The smaller of the two Republicans whispered an interjection," Tell him if we lose this load his head will swing for it!"The threat of a bullet in the head loitered in the air like burnt smoke. "Keep your voices down", the priest asserted.

Intelligence was the key, Michael Collins knew that. The systematic killing of Tan leaders and paid informers on a very bloody Sunday wreaked havoc with the British plans. Create bloody mayhem was Collin's intention and so one war was over and a new war began. Informers were everywhere, moles and counter moles on both sides living off scraps of information that led to wanton murder. Owen was aware that dozens of the Royal Irish Constabulary, believed to be in bed with Westminster, had been ambushed coming out of the pub, at their front doors, or walking to church. Sometimes they were the closest of friends, a neighbour or a shopkeeper. It was driven by fear and stealth, and no-one was safe. So, he wondered, why are they meeting now? What are they planning? Who will die tonight? They were not here to see Matt that was for sure. Anger coloured Owen's thoughts. Why wasn't he told of the plans? He was old enough. Old enough to die for his country. He didn't expect Joe, his step father to tell him, but why was his mother silent? In the background he could hear the rasping breaths of his younger brother coming from the next room and a deep, silent sigh filled his body. His brother, or more rightly his half -brother was barely six years old, Owen was almost ten years his senior. Owen pulled back the bed clothes and stood unashamedly half-naked, turned and nodded to Connor O'Donnell, the face now standing at the bottom of the bed. Connor gave him a respectful wink but said nothing. Connor had however, noticed even in the darkness of the room a series of faint bruises running across Owens's back. Connor looked down and gritted his teeth as if reminded of some past troubled feeling. "Where's Joe" said Owen looking searchingly at Connor as he fiddled for his under vest. Con was a big man with a ready laugh, always a good, near neighbour and friend to his mother in the past, but lately had kept himself to himself. Owen liked Connor and Connor's father Liam. It had been a while since Owen had seen Liam and for half a moment he wondered why. Come to think of it has anyone seen Liam? Connor had known his father well, though it frustrated Owen that for all these years he had said so little about him. "He's tucked up in bed." Connor nodded suddenly serious.

"Pissed you mean!" Con raised his eyebrows, taken aback by the anger in Owens's voice and though he knew Owen was physically and mentally mature above his years, was still surprised that one so young should speak this way. He would have squared up to Owen if things had been different but tonight he needed to be careful.

"Sleeping it off in the barn" said Con looking down and not wishing to make matters worse than they already were. "Thought so," said Owen broodingly tight-faced, silently thinking what father gets drunk when his only child is fighting for his life.

9

"Don't speak of Joe like that. He's your step- father now" said his mother in a retreating voice, all the laughter now gone. In that moment she wanted to take back the words, hold him tight and explain, but she couldn't tell the terrible thing she had done. Instead she threw a side comment to the solicitor, who seemed to offer comfort, placing a hand on her shoulder. Owen loved her dearly, more than he cared to admit to himself. What had happened to the mother he knew? She seemed strangely defensive tonight as if events were unfolding that she had little control over. Where was the once confident, outgoing person he had known as a child? His mother played absent mindedly with the strings of her apron like a set of rosary beads.

"Step-father, my da is dead" Owen responded quietly, shying away from wanting to fight with his mother. He knew how much she missed his father. He missed him too. That much they shared. Owen continued "You bring him home Con?" Connor merely nodded, anxious to let the conversation drop. Owen held his gaze. Connor uncharacteristically offered an explanation.

"Aye Owen, found him on the road by O'Leary's farm gate and carried him here. I knew your muther'd be worried." Con O'Donnell, known for his gentle, quiet ways, was built like a mountain and while Owen had never heard him lose his temper he dreaded the moment he would. Owen nodded in thanks but wished he had left his step-father where he had found him. He was lucky, that remnants of the Black and Tans still operating, had not found him first. They had been checking the roads around O'Leary's farm for the past few days. The talk that O'Leary was gun- running must be true. Thoughts slipped through his mind. Joe would have got a good kicking if they found him first. Even worse he'd be dead if the Auxiliary Squad was around. Bloodied in the Great War, these wayward squadies failed to settle back into normal life and metered out their own justice to all who fell in their path. The Tans would have got more than they bargained for if they'd caught Connor. Thoughts raced again. Was Joe gun-running as well? Connor did well to carry Joe all that way and avoid the Tans. How did he do it? Was there not a curfew? Owen shook his head and reviewed his thoughts. The Tans must have moved on? But it wasn't true.

This however was not the moment to annoy Connor for deep down it was dawning on him what he had to do and it unnerved him. His mother had already arranged his clothes at the foot of the bed and he dressed quickly. "Where will the doctor be?" said Owen looking up as he finished buttoning up his cotton shirt and cuffs.

"In the old pharmacy, he has arranged a number of extra beds and nursing support," his mother explained, "if you can count Eilleen M'Cleod that overblown protestant, as nursing support. God help us all!" Her voice rising with indignation and for one fleeting moment seemingly to become the mother he once knew.

"Ma," Owen took her two hands and looked into his mother's tired eyes. He saw the bottled up hurt and distress and mixed with confusion and helplessness. It had been a tough six years since his father died and said, "It will take some time there is a good distance to go."She composed herself before answering, "I know," she said in a low indistinct voice, "I know, God be with you. Now are you clear about the way, it's a bad night out there". She fastened and refastened one of the buttons on his shirt as she spoke.

Owen nodded, "I'll be fine. Don't fuss," he said, knowing his heart was pounding faster and faster.

All the time Owen contemplated the task ahead. He had run the six miles to Kilshanny across the moor many times but never at two o'clock in the morning, never in the pitch-black and never in the September rain. But he kept his doubts to himself. Father Ryan came over, "Owen. Are you ready for what you must do?" He had a featureless face for a priest. It was hard to judge his feelings but he had an easy, sugary way of talking. A transient smile, almost a snigger, slipped across his mouth.

"I am Father". Owen added, looking down, without making eye contact, aware he was talking to a powerful man. A powerful man who in Owens's eyes callously manipulated men and women, about money and sex, and living and dying. The priest leaned over and whispered in Owens's ear, "It's been a busy night, but take my advice, forget what you have seen and heard tonight and concentrate on helping your brother. We are about your father's business." Owen did not let his shock register on his face, but raised his head gave the priest a hard stare. What are you up to? Frantic thoughts slipped through his mind. What is a priest doing, mixed up in killings? But priests had been mixed up in killings ever since time

12

began. Maybe he knew about the ambush for Michael Collins? After all, it only happened but ten miles down the road. It wouldn't surprise him, sadly nothing surprised him anymore. "It's as good as done Father." said Owen, steadfastly, knowing that the priest had just told him to keep his mouth shut or face the any consequences. What has Joe got us into? He almost responded, disgusted with Joe's weakness. He continued to dress and slipped on his well worn linen jacket that his mother had brought in, put on his peaked cap and laced his ankle high boots, but before he made his way down the narrow uncarpeted stairway to the kitchen, he looked in on Matt. He pulled the linen collar of his jacket across his mouth before entering. The room was almost bare except for the cross of the crucifixion above the bed and some rudimentary curtains. A large basin of hot, steaming water, which his mother had used to wipe down his face and body, rested on the large corner window sill, now left a thick mist across the cold glass. But Matt, his six year old brother showed all the signs of diphtheria, the rasping voice, the sweaty pallor to the skin, the "bull neck" swelling of the lymph glands around the throat. He had struggled at first but then began to rally. But now he looked so much weaker. "God bless you Matt" he whispered to himself, for he knew time was running out, it would not be long. The enormity of the task made him feel nauseous.

The table in the kitchen was covered in half empty tea cups, the remains of the meeting. Thirteen cups in all he counted. So some have left? Owen calculated. The Irish flag green, white and orange lay draped across a chair.

Owen noted a half open road map with O'Leary's farm circled and a series of markings at intervals along the dirt track leading to the back of his farm. He picked out two crosses high up on the slopes above the farms outbuildings. Are these caves? He thought. He couldn't loiter long, feeling he was being watched. The two shadowy Republicans had brushed past him as they made their way outside to smoke and talk. One returned and hastily began to fold away the map and clear the debris on the table. Owen fiddled with his jacket to cover his nerves and made his way to the slatted farm door. Before he left, he hurriedly bit into an apple and swigged down half a cup of the milky, well sugared tea, grabbing a small walking stick made by his father, as he passed through the back door to the farm. "You be careful out there", he heard Connor shout as the farm door closed behind him. The Republicans stood with their backs to him, one urinating up the side of the barn. Out in the night his eyes quickly grew accustomed to the shadows of the farmyard and he made his way passed the barn banging with his walking stick on its large panelled door loud enough to wake the dead and the pissed, and up the pathway leading to Galteemore, the three thousand foot summit that rose majestically above the farm. The Galtee Mountains were part of a golden vale running across the counties of Limerick, Tipperary and Cork. He had walked the Galtees ever since he could remember and had scaled the heights of Carrignabbinnia and Slievecushnabbia with his father and delighted at school to spell their names with ease. He loved the wind-swept, stony, screed covered summits, intermingled with lush riverbanks and pine-forested hills. The wild flowers along the paths were always luxuriant, changing with the seasons. The sea-pinks and golden trefoil spectacular with blue cornflowers prominent in the mid-summer sun, gave way in autumn to Western Dwarf gorse, which carpeted the rough ground and mixed with purple heather made his journey, now so much more dangerous.

He had no idea why he had grabbed the small walking stick, before leaving, except as a spur of the moment drumstick, but as he began to run he felt comforted on this night to have it with him. There were a number of routes he could take to Kilshanny village, and as he ran strongly up the hill he began in his mind to map out the quickest way to the pharmacy. Though Matt was his half-brother he loved him dearly, but above all he knew what Matt meant to his mother. He knew that since his mother had remarried he had been pushed out of her life as if she could not bear to be with him any longer. He wondered selfishly if this was a chance to redeem him in her eyes. He knew he had no time to spare. To follow the roads would take longer. The quickest route lay across the moors, along the narrow foot-worn track across the cliff top leading to Buffers Cross, past the ruined windmill, before crossing the Armagh Bridge, past the Tincurry Workhouse, into the wood above Kilshanny. Once through the woods he would have a clear run to the pharmacy on the edge of the village. The route was dangerous and he knew it but he settled to the run and his rhythmic breathing calmed his nerves.

Much as the outdoors brought freedom and contentment, when walking or running the moors his thoughts always centred on his father and tonight strangely was no different

15

.His anger over his stepfather consumed him. He felt anchored by the past. Why did his mother have to marry such a fool? What was going on? He had never seen so many people at the house, not since his father's wake. Why did the priest say they were about his father's business? Did he mean Joe? It was well known that his father, Edmund, was an activist. Was he involved in killing people? He wanted to say no but quite simply he did not know. Everyone knew he had returned unexpectedly from the American continent ,six years ago, not having taken his priest hood training but with wealth enough to buy a farm, a public house and had enough over to invest in a newly established local Creamery. Owen knew he had benefitted from this newly acquired wealth and somehow it bothered him, as if it was wrong to take it. Such wealth opened doors however, and enabled Edmund, his father, to take Owen out of the local hedge school and send him to the newly built Christian Brothers academy where he excelled. Not for him, Owen thought would he any more remain tied to a hedge school like other Irish farmers' sons, meeting in a field by a hedge to be taught by better educated locals. But it was all short-lived. Within a year of his father's death, unable to manage the demanding needs of farm and public house, his mother had remarried. She was not a business woman and seduced by Joes promises of a prosperous future she put his drunkenness to one side. She had chosen poorly. What had Joe imagined he could achieve? For within three further years, with Matt born, the drunken fool had brought them to the brink of ruin. The public house was taken over by his father's brother Uncle John and the investment in the Creamery was sold off. Owen never knew why his Uncle John was involved. All that was left was the farm and a bleak future dependent on good weather. During that year they had all grown to live with hunger. As Catholics they had been subjugated for decades, no vote, and discrimination over work but since his father's death the hunger had been the worst. Being forever locked into a Westminster Parliament for decades had ensured that the only work for Catholics was farming what meagre land there was and certain starvation if the crop failed. To top it all the Catholic Church in all their wisdom had forbidden integration with Protestants. You couldn't even marry your way out of poverty. Strangely the Catholics of the north continually looked to the south as the Promised Land. But they were wrong, subjugation was everywhere. As the Gaelic League lamented, even to send a stamped letter meant licking the arse of the King. Owen had learnt the rules very quickly with his stepfather. Do as you're told or take a beating. Owen thus found himself on the hedge row again, until his wealthy 'Uncle John', Edmund's brother and as an acknowledgement of the regard he had for his dead father, agreed to pay for his education to continue. Owen had little idea of how that came about, but always wondered where his Uncle John got his wealth from. He was welcomed back by the Christian Brothers, who recognising the quality of the boy, and sensing that his Uncle John knew if Ireland was to achieve its greatness, it needed all the scholars it could get. Owen wondered what the pay back would be, but he studied well and immersed himself in all that he remembered about his father, especially the Land Act which he knew by heart. His father, Edmund was an impressive man, who commanded attention and people warmed to his manner and passion and talked of him as the new Parnell. Even Michael Collins respected him.

Charles, Stewart Parnell as he was known, was an early nationalist leader and land reform agitator, who had single-handedly changed the face of Irish politics. Not bad for a protestant thought Owen. It was his father that had given Owen that quality of maturity, the instinct to speak up, the alertness to act, the hunger to learn and the belief that luck favoured the brave. His father was born on the day of the Cambletown Massacre. For on September 9th of that year 1887, John Shinnick, John Casey, and Michael Lonergan were shot by police whilst breaking up a Land League Meeting called to organise a rent strike at the estate of Lady Kingston. As the shots rang out in the square in the village, his father's first infantile cries punctured the Cambletown air. At his every subsequent birthday the Cambletown Massacre was celebrated. His father grew up in heated discussions as the Battle of the Boyne was fought anew every day. But his father became intoxicated by the passion of his countrymen, the desire to resolve the inequalities of Irish society became the centre point of his life. At a young age he became a local voice, a town councillor, a friend to many, a staunch advocate and defender of the working man. He had a farmer's heart and a banker's knowledge, for some men have an eye for horseflesh, and some have an eye for risk, and Edmund had an eye for both. Nobody kept their head better, when markets were falling and weeping men were standing in the streets tearing up their letters of credit. On many occasions he had stood in church halls, on park benches rallying the locals to stand up for their Catholic rights and their ownership of the land. When markets were volatile, a number of farmers were indebted to him for arranging loans, but also for making their farms pay better.

Sometimes he was able to cut through the legal entanglements. Few could out talk him. For his efforts, he had twice been badly beaten by the Black and Tans and carried the name "The Campaigner". And he, Owen, was 'The Campaigner's' son. What footsteps will I leave? Owen pondered.

Owen did not remember how he had reached the top of Poulafreestone Hill. His leggings were now wet and covered in mud. He had somehow surmounted the one thousand and fifty three feet and had stood on its summit, wondering how he had got there without incident. He stopped for a moment. He breathed easily. His eyes had now become well accustomed to the dark and despite the lashing rain he could just make out the ruins of Buffer's Cross windmill way below. He was becoming soaked through and in the breeze was beginning to feel the cold of the night. Lightning was flashing and breaking on the horizon and his body shuddered with the arrival of another thunder clap echoing across the Glen of Ahernow. His mouth felt dry so he took two more bites of the apple that his mother had slipped into his jacket pocket and made his way down to the river. He sensed the tiredness in his body and the pressure on his knees as he made his descent .He had made good time, taking he thought about half an hour to reach the top. He prayed Matt was hanging on. He could not die. And he could not die not like his father. His mother would be devastated. His father had died, a few months after the Great War in March 1918; in the prime of his life, and like Michael Collins at just thirty –one years old. He was fit and able and like Parnell seemed to have been felled by the common cold. Owen had known from an early age, and had   come to understand that death is indiscriminate. For he was to later to find that unlike Parnell who died of pneumonia his father was an early victim of the Spanish Flu Epidemic so   called because King Alphonso of Spain also contracted the virus. But the old King had survived whereas his `much younger father had died just thirty -one years old. He also found through reading that a Harry Elionsky an American champion long distance swimmer, and Irma Cody, daughter of Wild Bill Cody, both young and fit people had also died alongside fifty million other poor, fit, young souls worldwide. His reading also informed him that Francisco De Paula Rodrigues Alves newly re-elected president of Brazil, also died before taking up his new office, poor sod thought Owen. Fate moves in mysterious ways. The names rattled through his mind like machine gun bullets.

The walking stick which had come in handy to steady his balance and haul himself over the boulder-strewn top of Poulafreestone Hill, was now becoming a disturbing weight to carry. He was disturbed also by his mother's behaviour since his father's death. She was so different with him when he left the farm, stiff and forever holding back. Why couldn't they talk anymore? He felt a small pang of comfort and delight in that she had slipped an apple without his knowledge into his pocket as he went out of the farm door. He didn't remember the embrace. Was it his fault? Was he holding back? But Matt he felt was her favourite. Matt was Joe's son, the first of the Cahill line, his half-brother and he Owen was the last of the Doyle's and as his father had told him, a true son of

Hibernia (as the Romans called Ireland).When Ireland belonged to the Irish.

Owen knew Matt had rekindled the hope in her, after his father's death, that life was worth living and for moments in the early days, she returned to the mother he once knew. He often wondered if she was still grieving. What had changed her he could not know? But she had not noticed in the intervening years how much she had spurned Owen's attention, not aware of their fading discussions, and the hardening of her expectations of him. She had not noticed that she had turned away when her new husband disciplined Owen. "He needs to be taught, Mary, he has a foul temper and by heaven I'll knock it out of him." Joe would tell her. And she had not noticed that Owen was more hurt by her indifference, than any wayward blows. But his anger was smouldering and growing, and as it grew, his love grew smaller. He waited for that moment of tenderness that never seemed to come and so the fire inside was never quenched. The anger drove him on down the hillside.

Owen slid past a huge boulder that marked the entrance to Buffer's Cross and the ruins of an old stone windmill. He was hardly out of breath. In earlier days this mill, uniquely driven by water and wind, had been the main source of milled wheat for miles around, even serving Cork city. It once had horizontal Norse paddles, a throwback to Viking domination. The turning force being produced by a channel of water, controlled by a sluice gate from the Funcheon River, causing the grinding stones to move against each other. It was also perfectly positioned to capture the south-westerly winds sweeping up the Glen of Ahernow. Having lived off the new technologies of wind and water for a century it failed to adapt to steam power and so was abandoned, being finally burnt down by revellers celebrating the passing of 'The Home Rule Bill' one wintry night. What was left of the mill now creaked and groaned in the wind, haphazardly shaking the remains of its sails, like some cabbage-white butterfly caught in a net. Owen crouched for a moment beneath the infinite mill sail and eyed the way across the river. The Bridge of Armagh was not a bridge, but a raised path made from stone. It rose from the river on three great boulders, and linking them together were three long stone planks about one and half feet wide. Wide enough for one person at a time to cross. It was a testing crossing, for one slip and the fast flowing Funcheon would carry the unlucky dipper rapidly down river. At night, in rain, in September it was more than an ordeal, it was a trial. What if he failed? What if he made a mistake? What if he had chosen the wrong route? What if he couldn't do it and had to return? What chance for Matt then?

He pushed the uncertainties to the corners of his mind and made his way past the mill towards the water's edge to carefully scrutinise the bridge. In parts green winter moss covered the stone and disturbing pools of falling rain welled on the surface. He looked for another way across but he knew in his heart that he was unlikely to find one, and so it proved to be. He had to walk the Bridge of Armagh if he was to get to the Kilshanny pharmacy. He edged past the mill window and his eyes caught the ringed carving of his father's and his own initials intertwined on the door and Owen smiled for the first time that night. He'd half-forgotten they were there but it brought back memories of a night camping under starlight, with his father, shortly before his younger sister was born. It was a night his father told him many things, for it was his father who had made him carry the name of Fanahan and it was a night he would never forget.

Owen knew it as a special name for it meant so much to his father so he carried and defended it against all comers. The name made him strong for names are everything in Ireland. Like cattle brands they burn indelible,unchangeable tattoos on the skin. They separate and define you. They carry five hundred years of fighting. Your secrets. Your history and origins. You are born with enemies and friends. On entering a room names create enemies you have never met and find friends you did not make. Your name buys a drink or a glass in your face. You're condemned before you speak and hailed as a hero without uttering a breath. For, they reveal who's Catholic or Protestant. They scream out if you're Unionist or Nationalist. Names get you cornered and boxed in. Names get you killed . Names get you a bullet in the head. Names even in death flatter your grave. Names like Fanahan are a passport to the next world. Owen was always careful who knew his name.

Owen knew of, but had no interest in Saint Fanahan, who was some hot tempered, warrior priest. He knew his father, as the third son , had left Queenstown and taken a steam ship to Liverpool to travel to the so called United States of America, to enter a seminary to become a priest.

He had the nagging question his father wanted him to become a priest? Owen felt the weight of these words in his heart. Would he ever be good enough? Priesthood was a celebrated event in the life of an Irish family. Even now he felt the need to honour his dead father's wishes. He took a deep breath trying to shed his frustration. Why did it matter so much even when his father was dead? Why had his father landed him with such a name? Fanahan was some killing, soldier priest, who like all priests wanted to control the world, Owen shrugged. The thoughts troubled him, like the continual splashes of rain across his face.

He knew he had a fiery temper but he was the first born and not the third son. He was ,by rights, destined to inherit the farm, Matt the second son would have to leave and some other unborn sod would become the priest. But would he inherit the farm or would his stepfather have other plans to give it to Matt? Who really owned the farm? Would the farm survive with Joe Cahill in charge? Would even Matt inherit the farm? Owen shook his head in confusion. His father had bought the farm but no-one really knew where the money had come from. His father had not even told his mother. A gift from God he would say. Having returned together from the United States of America, Edmund had set up as a merchant, and nothing was said about his priesthood, only stories abounded. What had happened? Some in the village, had thought he had become mixed up with the Irish extremists in America, the Cana Gael? Some believed that the money had come through crime. Some joked he had even stolen the Irish Crown jewels? Speculation was rife but his father was silent.

With all this anger and confusion rattling round his head he placed his foot on the topside of the stone bridge and brought his full weight to bear. He noticed immediately how swollen the river was, riding so high on the boulder pillars. Standing tall he took several steps forward till his leading foot slipped sideways on the green moss, but he kept his balance and steadied himself, remaining still for a moment. He reached the half way point and swayed, he could not go back. He knew he could not stay too long otherwise he would lose his nerve. He pushed on, slipping his feet forward like the tight-rope walker he had seen at the circus as a child, and using his walking stick to balance his weight. The unevenness in the surface was deadly and just he as thought he would make it, his feet slid away underneath him. His cry vibrated against the night and drifted unheard across the hills and moor. His legs entered the cold, freezing, surging waters and he felt himself being dragged down stream when he realised the walking stick he was still holding had wedged itself in a fissure in the stone bridge and he stopped with a jolt. Water cascaded over him and a sense of both dread and determination gripped his being. He pulled and pulled and the walking stick held. He inched his way back towards the bridge and lay still for a fraction of a moment to catch his breath, as he grasped the stone planks with his bare hands. With a final surge he placed his feet on solid ground at the end of the stone bridge. His breathing calmed with relief for he knew crossing here had saved a great deal of time, but at what expense. While he squeezed the water from his clothing, he had one last try to remove his walking stick, but it would not budge. His leggings were soaked through and the linen jacket weighed heavily on his shoulders, but more worrying he was incredibly cold. He visibly shivered for the first time since leaving the farm. Owen knew he had to move on quickly and so looking westward towards the dip in the hills he made his way down the slope towards Kilshanny village. He hoped the doctor was still there.

He hadn't been in the woods long when he heard movement in front of him. A twig snapped and he looked over his shoulder to see lights flickering through the trees. Some instinct inside him made his legs begin to run headlong into the woods. He began to panic. Before he knew it he was running and falling and when he fell, he scrambled along the ground trying to rise to his feet. His hands flicked brambles and ferns and tree trunks and drew blood. He ran till the lights faded and stopped for a breather by a large oak tree. Who in God's Heaven was out in the woods at this time of night? Then he laughed, you are you idiot! He brushed the blood, intermingled with rain, off the back of his hands and moved off. Looking back, he could see lights drifting eastward across the valley, towards the Armagh Bridge. Not wishing to delay, Owen turned towards Kilshanny and the satanic outline of the Tincurry Workhouse loomed like some vast, derelict mansion in the distance. It was a familiar sight, where he had met some of the inmates at the hedge school. This was the place where Marian lived. He had known her and her family before she was incarcerated into the workhouse after her parents died. He felt he knew her from the moment he saw her. Her easy manner made him laugh. There was something in her green eyes, that drew him in and made his heart jump. But Marian as he was to find out, had a mind of her own. The Workhouse now took on a strange aura, and he was surprised to see that lanterns had been placed against the two immense stone pillars that held the two cast iron entrance gates. Atop of the pillars were two giant stone-carved gargoyles, rampant like lions, enough to frighten off any unwanted visitor. This Children's Workhouse, now occupying the remains of the old Brookfield factory buildings, was originally set up by the Clogheen Poor Law Union during the height of the Great Irish Famine, to reduce overcrowding in Clogheen village. It was a terrible place to live and he feared for Marian's safety. Overgrown with yew and ash trees, the building, often pervaded with the cries and screams of inmates, appeared silent and still as Owen reached the cobbled forecourt at its entrance. Despite the lights set high on the entrance pillars the building appeared eerily quiet, and not daring to find out why, Owen made his way earnestly towards the pharmacy. The shadows wavered and rocked sending a mental shudder through his mind. He glanced backwards onl y to be dazzled by a burst of lightning that that danced across the gargoyles, which seemingly flapped their stony wings . Turning forward he ran on, sensing a set of cloven hooves pounding up behind him. He felt the merest touch of contact across his back and not daring to turn to face his assailant, his mind screamed. Banshee! Banshee! The scream seemed to come from some primeval place deep inside of him and for the first time Owen felt fear. He ran, and for the second time that night his legs seemed to buckle underneath him and arms flailing he skidded to a heap and lay for a fleeting moment still, before he felt his body slide of its own accord further down. He gathered speed on the slippery muddy surface and came to a sudden stop crashing into a dry stone wall .He did not know how long he lay there for, but gradually he began to sense the world again, and rose unsteadily to his feet. It was then he noticed the cow stood close by .He clenched his fists in anger, you stupid fool it was a cow. He reproached himself, but knew whatever time he had lost could not be caught up. He ran on.

The Georgian fronted building with Pharmacy written in white appeared ahead. Owen rattled the knocker. As Fiona M'Cleod opened, the blue panelled door and Owen overcome by the great sense of relief fell through the opening to the stone floor. Fiona recognised him instantly. "Owen? Owen ,what have you done to yourself ? Gently lifting him up and patting his face. "Doctor! Doctor Lewis! Hurry please!" The Doctor appeared, half dressed, sleeves rolled up, mask around neck, that could not hide the drawn, overworked eyes desperate for sleep.

"Owen? What's the problem?" the doctor inquired as he placed his stethoscope on the table.

"Leave him a minute, He's wet through! My God, he's run from the farm!" Fiona intervened, shaking her head. She helped Owen to sit upright against the pharmacy counter and began to wipe the blood off his face with a wet cloth.

"It's alright nurse Fiona there's little time," Owen in broken breaths looking from face to face added, "It's Matt he's worse". The doctor shook his head ," How

28

long Owen?", said the Doctor pulling a well-used black leather bag from the shelf above Owens's head and began to fill it with small glass bottles. The bottles clinked as he placed the bag on the pharmacy's flag floor ."What time is it?" Owen responded."Ten past four, "Fiona added, looking at the clock over the counter as she continued to clean the blood off his hands.

"It can't be!" He felt confused and angry. "It's taken me two hours I should have made better time than that."

"You've had quite a fall judging by the bruise on your face", Fiona said sympathetically. Owen felt his face as if trying to recapture the memory of what happened. "I was chased by a cow I remember that", but the rest was hazy .

By now Doctor Lewis had put on his great coat and made his way out of the back of the pharmacy. Whilst Owen readied himself retying his laces and adjusting his clothing, Doctor Lewis had brought round his pony and trap to the front of the pharmacy. He handed Owen a loose blanket. The pony chomped on a bag of hay placed over its head. The two wheeled trap, barely wide enough for the two of them with Fiona having squeezed the vital medical bag between them, lurched forward barely fifteen minutes after Owen had knocked on the pharmacy door. Owen felt tiredness overtake him and with the rocking motion of the trap, he nodded off to sleep intermittently until Doctor Lewis gently shook his shoulder. His instincts kicked in as he recognised the half - ploughed meadow, laid to potatoes on the edge of his father's farm. They had made good time and within fifty minutes they reached the entrance to the farm. The house was in darkness with no signs of its previous visitors still around, save a small fluttering light. Owens's dog greeted the arrival of the trap as Connor O'Donnell opened the door. He was stony-faced. "It's not good Owen",

"What do you mean? The Doctor's here!" His eyes flashed white.

"Owen it's too late", said Connor looking directly at Owen and stretched out his arm. Connor's voice grew lower and more intimate."Owen it's too late." Something in the glint of Connor's eyes signalled a reaction in Owen and the awful truth dawned. "It can't be," Owen said feeling devestated.

"It's too late, Matt died just twenty minutes ago," Connor added in a low voice which dwindled away to nothing ,as if he by not saying, it could not be true. The words pierced Owens's body like stone icicles and he stopped dead unable to comprehend what had happened. He tried to speak but no sound came. He looked round for his mother. She sat motionless in the fireside chair staring into the remains of the fire. Her face was covered in tears and rigid with grief. She did not respond to his presence. As Owen turned towards her, Joe Cahill's voice rang out. "You did this! You couldn't wait to bring me down! You didn't care for your brother! You killed your brother to get at me! You want the farm! You took his life for a few measly acres."

Owen struggled to understand what was meant .He took his mother's hands. "It's not true! It's not true!" The anguish in Owens's voice resonated across the room. But his mother did not move. As if in a world of her own, the jigsaw of the shapes and sounds of the room were merely an irrelevant background to her loss, and she never took her eyes off the fireside flames. "You ungrateful sod", rang in Owens's ear as Joe Cahill pressed his face eyeball to eyeball with him. Owen could smell the dark stench of beer and the farmyard excrement from sleeping in the barn. Two powerful hands hauled Owen upwards, but Owen didn't care. He held onto his mother's hands but she didn't respond and he found himself being dragged out of the farmhouse door. With a violent swing Owen was hurled through the door and landed on the limestone paving at the front of the farm. Joe Cahill was on him in seconds, a brutal kick caught Owen across the chest and he fell back winded. Doctor Lewis cried out. Owen clasped his head and braced himself for the next blow to fall but it didn't come. Amid all the noise and voices, the shouts and the screaming, all of which was a white blur to Owen, he suddenly realised Connor O'Donnell had felled Joe Cahill with an almighty blow to the head. Joe Cahill staggered back, astounded not only at the unexpectedness of the blow, but also the immense power of it and he fell to the floor trying to stem the outpouring of blood from his nose and mouth. "On his side are yer", he said spitting blood.

"I'm on no one's side but if it means stopping you doing something you'll regret then I'm ready", said Connor wondering if he had done the right thing.

31

"Calm down Joe, "the Doctor pleaded, "The fights over",

"Stay out of it Doctor this is between me, the boy and Connor. It's not over till I say so. Where's he been? Why did he take so long? Come on Connor ask the question!" Connor looked towards Owen.

"I'm sorry Connor I'm struggling". Owens's mind was a blur and only bits seemed clear.

"Which way did you go", Joe blurted forth.

"Across the Armagh Bridge", replied Owen trying to recover his composure.

"Liar! There's just one catch", said Joe smiling in victory. "The Armagh Bridge was washed away earlier tonight. The river overflowed .We were informed by the Garda earlier in the evening, they have been out looking for three boys who absconded from Tincurry Workhouse. They combed every inch of Kilshanny woods and never saw you." In addition, he gave a bitter laugh. A fleeting vision came back to Owen when he realised the flickering lights was a search party looking for the boys. Owen suddenly remembered," My walking stick is trapped on the bridge", and his voice tapered off, as he realised that any evidence to back his assertions would be probably washed half way across the Irish Sea by now.

"You stay away from my house, you hear me", Joe Cahill threatened. "Your house! My father's house!" The words screamed in silence in Owens's head. Connor recognised that no further discussion was possible

32

tonight and was determined to have no more trouble. Owen regained his feet and stood up straight. Connor looked across to Joe and explained "I'll take Owen with me but tomorrow we sort this out."

"It'll be a pointless visit, he's not coming back"

"That's not all your decision", said Connor but Mary Cahill had still not come to the door. He put his arm round Owen and they moved off in the direction of O'Leary's farm. The Doctor patted Connor on the back as he left, and went to attend to Joe Cahill. Owens's sister woken by the noise appeared at the door and Owen glancing back gave a small wave. Tears fell. For she had heard Joe's words and she knew he meant it.

Connor set off at a brisk pace, but they walked comfortably side by side, even though he knew Owen was tired; he needed to get him into the warmth of his cottage as soon as possible. Owen was quiet, deep in thought and cradled his arms around his upper body for warmth as he walked. He couldn't remember ever feeling so cold. As they neared, Connor's home the sky brightened with moonlight and in the distance the muted peel of the Clonmel church bells played across the valley. Owen looked up was surprised to see that the fields of Connor's farm had remained unploughed. There was little discussion between them except Connor enquired. "So when you slipped off the Armagh Bridge it was your father's stick that saved you?" He paused. "It's probably washed down river by now". Owen offered. It was clear that they'd both had the same thought. Owen nodded in silence, he could not forget the look on his mother's face and he carried these thoughts into Connor's house. The house was warm and Connor threw a log into the old cast-iron stove in which a fire had been lit earlier that day, and it sprang into flame immediately. As Owen started to remove his wet clothes, Connor reappeared with a towel, leggings and a shirt."They maybe a bit big", he said "but they're dry", nudging Owen with his arm trying to bring a smile to his face. Connor had rustled up a large cup of sweet, dark tea and a piece of buttered bread. Owen took them with thanks. "We'll have a good breakfast in the morning", and then added with some resolve, "We'll need it". Owen took a swallow of the hot tea, but was strangely disinterested in food. He played with the buttered bread and attempted a mouthful. His side ached from Joe's kick and he longed for sleep, fatigue was overcoming him rapidly. Connor's cottage was well proportioned but sparsely furnished, and he pointed Owen towards two narrow doors, which led to two smaller rooms, each containing a bed. Connor had done well to make the place habitable from the shell that had existed before. "Either one. here ", Connor shouted and handed him a candle. Owen settled for the first on the left. Before he entered the bed room he placed his hand on Connor's shoulder and looking down said, "Thank you," and with that pulled the door closed behind him. It was a small bedroom with a narrow double bed, a bedside table and a wardrobe, probably handed down through the family. He placed the half -full cup on the bedside table and rested for a moment on the side of the bed. Blowing the candle out he sat for a while in the darkness, his mind a blur of thoughts. He suddenly felt

34

lonely and uncertain. He couldn't get the picture of his mother out of his mind. Had she disowned him? How could Matt have died? Where is the God who protects us? I tried so hard he murmured to himself. He gripped the blanket in both his fists and tried not to let the rising emotion overpower him. Carefully, stiffly he rose from the bed and tried to straighten up. Every part of him hurt. He struggled to remove his wet shirt and shrug off his anger. He said to himself this would not happen anymore. This was the last time any man would hit him. He didn't want revenge, but somewhere in their meetings Joe had not understood Owen. For Owen had already admitted to himself he didn't know what made Joe tick. He tried to bury these thoughts as he laid his head on the pillow .He was old enough to know that no matter how good his relationships were, it was no guarantee of love and affection. Family he now knew from experience is mostly in the mind and sometimes proximity is lethal. How could all this have happened? Tragedy was stitched into all he touched like a heavy black sadness. He had begun the night in his muther's bed and ended the night in a stranger's bed and in between, chaos and death had fallen. He above all had learnt on this night, on the eve of his dead father's birthday, at the tender age of sixteen , the final rules of engagement of Irish life. There is no sanctuary. None shall be given and none must be asked for. You are either for or against. There are no in-betweens. If he is for his brother, he is against his sister. For in this life, whatever he wanted he would have to fight for everything, and against everyone. He must fight his family. He must fight his friends and destroy his foes.

All that was certain was the struggle. So it was him `against his brother, but his brother was no more. So it was him against his step-father because his father was no more. His stepfather and him against the Catholic Priest. The Catholics against the Protestants. The Nationalists against the Unionists. And everyone against the English and the Black and Tans. For he had decided even though he was the Campaigner's son, even though he was a true son of Hibernia, that when the time came, as soon as he was able, he would leave Ireland forever.

Chapter 2

Liverpool Docks November 1906

'The Third Son'

Edmund sat, with his back to the winter sun, in a small almost deserted outdoor working man's cafe overlooking Liverpool docks. He glanced across the waters to the Mersey Docks and Harbour Board Offices, now occupying the newly erected Edwardian Baroque style building clad in Portland stone. The large dome atop of it's grandiose rectangular structure was like some vast observatory destined to watch the comings and goings of all the flotsam of the world. He held his head in his hands, elbows splayed out, across the table. His face carried a contented smile. He was excited and nervous, wanting to get on, frustrated with the waiting. "Is she not a beautiful ship Liam?" Liam was Edmund's best friend from an early age, though he was a good five years older. He was married with a young son called Connor. Liam was preoccupied with his own thoughts, but nodded, not quite knowing if it was a question or a statement. Liam was wondering if it was the right time to leave Ireland when he threw a thought into the conversation.

"Is this not strange Ned, here we are, you and I ,travelling all the way to New York city and Eamon De Valera , an unknown, silver-spooned Irish American, has travelled all the way from New York to live in Dublin. When are we going to get someone home-grown?"

Edmund looked across the table. He knew what Liam was really saying. Why was he not putting himself up for political office? Why was he even thinking of becoming a priest? But what can a third son do? He answered directly putting an end to any further inquiry. "We need work. There's no work in Ireland. He needed a country to fight for. Good luck to him. Our turn will come."

Liam shrugged, knowing if you are Catholic, even a master builder could not find work "You're right we need work. It would be good to work again. Will the Five Points be good to us, that's the question?"

Edmund nodded slowly, "We will get work. I will use my brains and you, your brawn." He teased the older man with a wink of an eye.

"Less of the brawn", Liam responded.

Edmund could see violent resistance was rising across the green fields. Irish Americans were finding increasing amounts of money to furnish guns and explosives but it was full of dangers. Not everyone liked the Irish as Edmund was to find out. He knew more about De Valera than he had let on to Liam. His conversations with Michael Collins had given him a detailed picture of De Valera, the smooth politician. Collins however had lived through the troubles which spurned in him a natural anger that could only lead to more deadly, armed conflict. For a moment he questioned himself was he really leaving to escape the violence? Did he really want to take sides? Was violent resistance the only answer? De Valera was cautious and a politician, the two aspects usually meant not much would ever get done?

"And as for Eamon De Valera, Michael Collins will sort him out." Michael Collins lived in the next village of Conakilty, but five miles away and was a close ally, but Edmund never realised how wrong he was going to be.

On the wooden table, frayed with use, lay a small hand-made rucksack and beneath it, with its edges, flapping in the slight sea breeze, a ticket bearing the green and white seal of the RMS Lucania. The ticket edges vibrated like ticker tape as if receiving a final message of farewell. Across the bay the Lucania, first of the classic liners, with its dark black hull and white superstructure topped with two great smokestack funnels newly arrived from New York, was taking its berth at Pier Head .Owned by Cunard, and built by the Fairfield Engineering Company, a winner of the Blue Ribbon, as the fastest passenger liner from Liverpool to New York, the Lucania exuded quality from bow to stern.

Two great blasts announced its presence to the other ships moored in the harbour. A crescendo of echoing blasts circled the harbour in greeting the new arrival. "You hear that Liam!" exclaimed Edmund, trying to get a response from his quiet friend. Moving alongside was the Shenandoah, an older lumbering liner weighing seven hundred and forty tons and provided a stark contrast to the elegant Lucania. "Well I'd hate to be going on that old death trap," said Edmund pointing with his eyes towards the Shenandoah. On the dock side waiting to fill its hold were two hundred prime cattle, which along with mature young men, were Ireland's biggest exports.

"I don't know," said Liam wondering what steerage held for them on the Lucania, "a ship is a ship." Edmund smiled refusing to have his enthusiasm dampened and sensing they were on the verge of another adventure was desperate to taste every minute of it. He lifted the mug to his lips and drained the last remaining cold dregs of bitter Camp coffee. He shrugged, as he preferred tea, but as he was going to New York, he figured he had better get used to drinking coffee. He pulled the green white ticket from under the rucksack and re-read the inscription. It was a one way ticket, steerage class heading for New York, due to leave at 3-00pm on the afternoon tide. He placed the ticket into the internal pocket in his rucksack alongside a small locket and a letter of introduction to the St Josephs Seminary and College, in Yonkers, New York and all the money he could scrape together, some 50 American dollars. St Josephs was the "west point" of all seminaries in New York and was nick-named Dunwoody after the district it was located in. Edmund knew his father and the priest had pulled a lot of strings to enable his entry into probably the finest seminary anywhere in the civilised world. He still wondered if he had made the right decision. His conversations with the priest and his father made him feel there was purpose in being a priest. Could it lead more easily to a political solution without the violence. But there was a wayward part of him, that he needed excitement and challenge. He felt the buzz and anticipation of new horizons. He knew he had to go, he had to see how it would play out.

Liam and Edmund had made their way to the Steerage Ticket Office on Queenstown docks in Ireland, to buy tickets for the voyage earlier in the previous day. It was a warm dry day with a stiffish, cold easterly wind blowing and the sun was low in the sky. But they were in high spirits. The steerage offices were located in a dingy basement of a large stone building just off the main passage way to the docks. Having descended twenty steps, they eventually entered a narrow dark corridor full of filing cabinets and wooden chairs stacked along the walls. An underground , basement smell took the place of the sea air. Unshaven officials passed them without speaking or even acknowledgement with their eyes. They began to hear a low murmuring of voices in the distance and came into a small, poorly-lit room with an office counter in front of them and some thirty or so fellow passengers standing in groups and around the walls. Though Liam and Edmund had arrived in time, the agent was no-where to be seen. A small silence fell as they entered the room and a flurry of concealed glances ran around the room, and then as if someone had clicked a switch, the low murmuring punctuated with excited laughter re-entered the room. They found a place to stand and tried to imagine where the queue started .On the arrival of the agent, they soon found there was no queue and a tense mêlée and slight chaos broke out until Edmund asked, "Shall we start the queue over here", and he motioned to the agent who was now ready to receive passenger requests, who nodded in appreciation. Some passengers rose to argue but the nod of ascent from the agent and the fact that Edmund continued with, "Has anyone waited an hour?" quelled their ardour. A few passengers raised their hands. "Would you like to come over here?"Edmund beckoned assertively. "Who do you think you are telling people what to do?" said a large stocky, unkempt gentleman sitting in prime position nearest the counter. Edmund could tell from his accent he was Scandinavian and met his gaze with a smile. "I'm moving for no-one", he challenged. Liam stepped forward and gave the man a heavy -lidded look. The man began to square up to Liam when Edmund intervened again. "It's alright Liam, the gentleman's quite right. Tell me sir have you been waiting long?" Liam relaxed very slightly to allow Edmund to play the game out. "Not long", said the gentleman beginning to feel the eyes of the crowd upon him. "Come sir," said Edmund with all the guile of a skilled speaker dealing with a heckler, "you can't deny these people have waited some considerable time." The man edged back unconsciously creating a space into which Liam stepped, adding pressure for the man to withdraw even further. "Well I suppose women and children should come first," and backed away to another part of the room. He whispered quietly under his breath to Edmund as he passed "Watch out for your back, Irish". Edmund smiled, having been threatened by Protestant Unionists on many occasions, and proceeded to organise the queue. An hour and twenty minutes later Liam and Edmund were the last but two to be processed. At the desk they were met with a checklist of questions .Were they married? Could they read or write? Had they been in prison? Were they polygamists? Who had paid their passage? Did they have more than thirty dollars? Where was their final destination? For some passengers going to the Eastern Seaboard States, had to pay for the onward rail travel as well. As Edmund and Liam answered the questions a young beautiful woman accompanied with a bright eyed child returned to thank them for their help. For a moment their eyes, his blue, hers green, met and then she was gone. The agent handed through their tickets allocating them to group F, telling them to be at the Landing stage at one o'clock the following day. The agent thanked Edmund for his help and nodded to Liam, letting them know he would see them right on board. Within the hour they left on the ferry to Liverpool.

Passengers were now beginning to disembark from the Lucania and the docks were suddenly filled with a stream of stewards and porters carrying trunks, cases, and boxes of all shapes and sizes. Edmund and Liam, by now were at the Landing stage in a good position to see the celebrities of the day being escorted down the first class passengers walk way. The daughter of an American steel magnate was the first to emerge. A great cheer rose from the swelling crowd followed by further sharp blasts of the foghorn and a shower of confetti and streamers from the first class passenger portholes. Smiling she acknowledged their welcome with a wave. Newly- weds Gaby Deilys and Harry Pilcer followed .Wearing a full length fur coat ,and black crepe hat with feather she stood and posed for photographers allowed on the first class passenger deck. Harry Pilcer emerged smoking a cigarette and pulled the unfastened velvet collar of his great coat round his shoulders. He looked every inch the banking financier and prompted his bride to make her way down the walk way. He was followed by two bellboys carrying two small, yellow, mottled alligator skin suitcases. Edmund instantly recognised the good looking, chisel -faced financier having followed his rise to millionaire status through the Irish Financial Times. Edmund had since a small boy shown a real acumen for maths and financial arrangements. He could calculate the odds on a horse race as he spoke. His father had made a living on it. He had followed the rise of the Irish economy, scrutinising the Dublin Stocks and Shares lists, charting the rise of the Wicklow Copper Company, noting the price of sugar in Ceylon, the cost of tallow, the sale of twenty thousand bales of cotton in the Liverpool Cotton Market and the failure of the Irish wheat market with the poor attendance at the Drogheda Corn Market. He did not have the money to invest but had practised with his own fantasy stock market funds, buying and selling shares and acquisitions, at one time going bankrupt and now nearing his first imaginary million pounds. He had learnt well and his interest and skills in maths and finance had given him an edge into the physical world which did not always bode well with his priestly intentions. And deep down Edmund knew it. Just as he was leaving Harry Pilcer turned to shake hands with Jimmy Clabby, the newly- crowned world boxing champion. A huge cheer went up from the crowd. Liam lamented the fact he was a Protestant and one day he hoped a real Irish man would be world champion.

With the last of the disembarkees moving off in the
distance, the huge crowd of eager travellers had
assembled on the Landing stage. They were from all
walks of life .Men in high-collared great coats, women in
heavily stitched jackets and tightly fitting head scarves,
young children with knapsacks over their shoulders, all
carrying stiff-sided suitcases and boxes tied with string,
and wearing a smile on their faces. They gathered in
hope and expectation, in awe of the technology of this
huge ship about to transport them across the world
.Almost as one this huge, winding caterpillar of
humanity began to surge like a wagon train up the
gangplank towards the middle deck entrance. A parade
of pursers and stewards ,prompted by bugle call and
dressed in white , waited like angels at the Pearly Gates
nodding and directing them, whether you were up or
down to heaven or to hell. Edmund reached the band of
angels first but his affable greeting fell on stony faces
and alongside Liam they were assigned to hell. The easy
going crowd suddenly became tense as it entered the
narrow, steep and dark entrance leading to steerage. The
travellers began to press on each other, bags became
trapped, children squeezed their mother's hand tighter
for fear of being left behind, people began to shout
profanities at each other and a wave of uncertain
anticipation swept the trail of bodies. By degrees, the
bags the boxes, the knapsacks and the bodies edged their
way down increasingly steep stairs to steerage. Edmund
felt this sense of foreboding and tried to support those
around him but he also became helplessly trapped and
the great snake slipped as one to the chasm below. The
sense of uncertainty turned to disgust as the air became

45

thick and a rising smell filled the space around them. A wide-eyed steward, poorly dressed, dismissive and desperate to leave, directed them according to their groups to various parts of their new home. They were met by a sea of double height iron beds running the whole length of the ship .Hell was never so neat. Like some great, imprisoning, iron grid it separated them male from female, home grown from foreigner .Edmund spied the girl with the green eyes unburdening her sister of the heavy knapsack. He smiled but she turned away. Edmund took a lower bunk and Liam the one above. He looked for a moment at the battered tin plate, well-used knife and fork scattered haphazardly across the stained straw mattress and then to Liam and they both knew it was going to be a hard crossing for the next twelve days.

Edmund looked back towards the green eyed girl and noted she had glanced in his direction and he smiled, she likes me he thought. As he wandered over, he caught the movement of the Scandinavian and a group of men in the foreigner's corner furtively talking. With the only light coming from the portholes he made his way slowly through the grid of beds. The beds were now covered in a strange assortment of debris, carpet bags, half-eaten food, clothes, strange looking bottles, fruit, a small doll, for this was the totality of all that was owned. Kneeling in front of him was the young girl."What's your name?" Edmund inquired. The elder woman turned round and before the young girl could answer, Edmund asked nervously, "How are you settling in?"

"We're fine, not comfortable but fine," she responded with her steadfast green eyes. "It's a bit of a hole", Edmund added.

"It's a big hole and one that's likely to get blacker, but I think we have access to the deck above each day," she added hopefully. Edmund noted how much better the women's quarters were than his."What are you doing here?" Edmund startled, spun round. "This is women only," and then as if to rub it in. "No men!" retorted a large full bosomed woman. "Sorry" said Edmund backing round and making a mental note not to stray too near to her bed at night. The green eyes shouted "Meet you on deck and held his gaze.

"I don't know your name?"Edmund shouted as he retreated from the glare of the older woman. "It's Mary" and mine is Edmund.. As he returned to Liam, Edmund felt he was being watched .The small band of foreigners and the Scandinavian turned their backs as he passed through. With a sudden lurch, the Lucania got underway and the escorting tugs peeled off with a sharp horn blast and the great vessel threaded its way through the harbour to the open sea. The Atlantic called. Groups of travellers rushed to the portholes to try to glimpse the last sight of their homeland. They stretched out their hands desperate to touch the last vestige of land and like spawning salmon, they wondered if they would ever return. In that moment they were severed from their past and blindly went forward with no vision of their future. When Edmund reached his quarter, Liam had already gone to reconnoitre the other areas open to those in steerage. Apart from the deck room and limited access along each side of the deckhouse, to the lower middle deck and the open air, there was no access to any other parts of the ship. Moreover from time to time parts of the area were roped off to stop steerage travellers from going too close to the saloon passenger windows.

Within a few hours of leaving port the air in steerage was filled with the smell of vomit. Many returned to their beds to lie prostrate and remedies and advice abounded on how to solve their sickness. Liam and Edmund, both good sailors, made their way to the middle deck and fresher air. Even here the smell of vomit intermingled with the smell of the cooked stew for the evening meal spiralled up from the depths of the ship. Only those with the strongest stomachs ventured to eat. Edmund and Liam had decided that whenever possible they would sleep on deck. They had found a piece of tarpaulin to protect them from the downward spray that sometimes fell across the middle deck. As the days passed more steerage passengers took the opportunity to sleep on deck to avoid a night of stale, thick air below.

On taking his bedding up one night, Edmund caught sight of Mary.. On meeting, he shook her hand and exchanged greetings, discovering that she and her sister Megan were going to join her brother and his wife, to help run their chandlers shop they had set up on the Hudson River Bay entrance to New York. For his part he explained his link to Dunwoody Seminary, and she remembered fleeting memories of an Irish man called the Campaigner. As the days went by, they began to meet regularly and occasionally Mary and Megan would also sleep on deck. Despite the joy, meetings with Mary would bring to his day, Edmund continued to have a sense of unease, of being watched and though he vigilantly scanned his surroundings he found no clear evidence that his discomfort was real or imagined.

The following morning a red sky poured in through the portholes. The wind had risen and the already white topped, choppy sea was pitching the Lucania from side to side. The iron gates had been closed and no-one could leave to seek fresher air. The wind coming through the portholes only served to drive in the damp and send an odour of unwashed and sick bodies around the steerage space. Adding to the nausea was the almost constant clanging of the steerage cables running below their feet. Many travellers returned to their beds, most lay, others sat in small groups playing cards or in hot discussion. Some accosted the wide-eyed steward who reluctantly brought more clean drinking water seasoned with raspberry vinegar, or lemon juice. Edmund put on his last clean shirt knowing he needed to wash.

Conditions at sea had worsened. The nights were filled with the groans of the sick and the quarrels and fighting that had broken out. The air was cluttered with the noxious, nauseating stench of tobacco smoke and urine, intermingled with vinegar diluted with sea water ,used to wash down the deck each day. During those first four days a young two year old boy had died of convulsions, and a traveller who spent most days drunk on laudanum and rum was placed in the lock-up. The young boy sewn into the blanket that once gave him warmth, and now became his shroud, was committed to the sea one rainy morning. For a moment, he floated clinging to the real world before his tiny body slipped beneath the waves forever. Reality suddenly hit the travellers that this was their first burial and that others would undoubtedly follow, and that for some their dream would be over before it had begun. The crew on the other hand, seasoned on burials at sea, having paid their respects, returned to their work.

It was on the sixth day at sea that events began to turn. It began as night rolled in with a thick freezing fog and even with the kitchen fires maintained at a high output, the temperature in steerage fell rapidly. Edmund had met with Mary on the middle deck as usual, close to the saloon passenger windows. They could hear the band in the first class, passenger lounges playing and the peel of melodic notes was like birdsong in the desert of sea. Mary was deep in thought. Edmund tentatively put his arm around her shoulder, not wishing to cause any impropriety. But she accepted his gesture naturally and rewarded his kindness with a kiss to his cheek. "Is Megan coping?" said Edmund

"She's not, she's not eating, can't seem to keep anything down", Mary replied putting a defiant face on it. She left momentarily to see how Megan was coping. On her return Edmund handed her some apples he had managed to buy from a fellow traveller.

As they returned below a few days later, a crowd of agitated travellers blocked their entrance. Edmund spotted Liam going through his belongings. " Oh no! What's going on Liam?" Edmund raised his eyebrow with slight concern, half guessing what had happened. "Someone's been thieving", Liam answered bluntly. "Check your bag, and you as well Miss Mary," looking across at her. There had been talk of a spree of missing small "things", a bag of fruit, some loose change, and a hairbrush that had rippled through steerage over the past few days. It was never quite clear if they were taken or lost. "Someone has taken all her money," as Liam exclaimed and pointed out a young woman across the sea of beds." How much?" said Mary hurrying towards her bed. "About thirty dollars", Liam answered. "Check your bags," Liam insisted again looking at Mary. Edmund felt through the small rucksack he had kept hidden under the straw mattress. He looked up annoyed and felt again, "They're gone", he said, "Someone has taken my letter of introduction to the seminary." "Someone's taken your letter of introduction," Liam repeated annoyingly as if not quite comprehending what Edmund had said. "Why would anyone take the letter?" Edmund looked in disbelief. "What about your money"

"Money's fine. I put it in my sock earlier. Had a feeling that something might happen but why take the letter?" Edmund silently cursed himself for not being more vigilant. His eyes looked up as a small faint cry came from the ladies quarters. "Mary? Mary?" Edmund queried as he and Liam moved towards the other side of steerage to her bed where Megan, still unwell, lay in a deep sleep. Mary looked at her bag and realised immediately that someone had disturbed all her clothing.

She frantically searched for a small red pouch and discovered it had been ripped open and its contents, all her money, save some loose change, had been taken. She stood still for a moment frozen in time, unable to take in the consequences of the theft. Edmund seeing all, broke the silence. "I'm so sorry", he murmured as he took in the immediacy of its impact. Mary gathered all her strength and gritting her teeth to maintain her steadfast attitude felt the tears roll down her cheeks. Edmund moved to hold her close and she sobbed in his arms."It will be fine", he blurted not really knowing what he meant, speaking only to console, as he couldn't bear to hear her cry. Megan began to stir and Mary slipped from his embrace and started to respond to her needs, as if to put this event out of her mind.

Edmund needed to clear his head and made his way to the middle deck. The deck was crowded with angry fellow passengers, men, women and children. Liam eventually followed, finding him close to the middle class passenger lounge. Great clouds of smoke poured from the funnels trailing behind the ship like some black feather boa. A flock of gulls circled like vultures overhead. "This is a bad business, Edmund."

"A strange one", Edmund responded. "I'm baffled. Taking the money I understand, but why take the Letter? Who-ever they are. It has no value except to me. Maybe they can't read and will return when they realise."

"The captain has ordered a search of crew and second class cabins and communal areas. Including here." Liam added.

"Good" said Edmund

"It might sort out the Scandinavians"

"And what about Mary?"

"Well," said Liam, "she will need money but it will now take weeks to get down the Hudson to her brother".

"Has she said what she will do," said Edmund staring out to sea.

"She's keeping her own council", said Liam, "Not sure if she's thought it through yet". Pulling his coat further around him.

"Can we help her?"Edmund knew what the answer would be but asked anyway.

Liam looked and nodded, "Careful how you put it, she's a proud lady"

"I know, I kinda like that ".Though the ship was only in its seventh day at sea, it seemed like weeks had passed. Another young child, a girl had died, the second death since the ship ploughed forth into the Atlantic. Edmund spoke to Mary that evening. At first she put up a strong resistance but reality eventually compelled her to accept Edmund's offer of support. "And the priesthood?" she enquired. "Will you pursue it", she asked awkwardly.

"I owe it to my father and the priest, Father Thomas. The College will force me to get another letter which will take weeks. In the meantime we will work. The Five Points will be our home for a while." Edmund grimaced at the thought. If half of what he had heard of the Five Points were true life was about to get very difficult.

When Liam and Edmund returned below quietness had come over the sea of beds. The family of travellers talked in hushed voices covering their speculations. For the mood had changed. The trust, what little there was, had gone and anger had taken its place. Passengers eyed each other with suspicion and doubt. The cardinal rule had been broken, never steal from the family. Liam and Edmund had talked of the possibilities and though the Scandinavians had figured in their discussions, Edmund felt that it was just too simple.

The depressed atmosphere continued for the next three days and everyone confined themselves to their own business. The wide-eyed purser flitted in and out of steerage like a meercat, half watching, and half listening as if waiting for some tragedy or triumph to break the silence. When it came it turned out to be both. That evening as Mary and Edmund wandered on the middle deck a young Hungarian woman, travelling with an older man, suddenly cried out in pain grasping Mary's arm as she fell to the deck. Instinctively Mary turned and softened the fall. She knew what was wrong instantly. Edmund looked aghast, "Great heavens has she broke her ankle?"

"No she's having a baby." The older man looked horrified.

"Can you 'elp her?" He stuttered in patois English.

"Get the purser! Get some hot water."Within minutes the screams grew stronger. Mary organised arrangements with all the skills of a midwife. As the travellers on deck watched in discreet awe, Mary with the help of two fellow travellers delivered not one but two baby girls. Loud cheers followed the first and even louder with the second. The excitement continued with a celebratory drink provided by a first class passenger who was elated by the arrival in his cabin of three Blenheim spaniels the off-springs of a dog owned by his mother. The triumph was upon them. It was now impossible for the travellers not to talk and celebrate. So they did. The grandfather carrying his new born grand-daughters was congratulated and patted as he escorted his daughter carried on a stretcher to the beds below. Something approaching normality began to return .Even those who had lost all their money realised that it was impossible not to speak or make contact in such a confining space. That evening Mary and Edmund paid a call to the young Hungarian woman and her new born water babes. The young woman and her father were ecstatic in their thanks .The father looked overwhelmed."I wish my wife be here to see such wonder."He breathed out. "Katchia." He looked at his daughter "We must repay these people. I am, how you say, alchemist."

"You're a pharmacist?"

"Yar pharmacist," the old man exclaimed with a beaming smile. "Can I help." Edmund knew what was needed and within the hour, poor Megan had her first dose of *nux vomic* a very mild strychnine compound that began to make Megan's life so much better.

The following morning, the ship's tannoy barked out the message that the Lucania had now entered American waters and would reach port in the next three days. The Duty officer also announced that they had quietly arrested the steerage purser last night who was now confined to his cabin. The news was met by silence and then uproar as questions abounded as to whether they would get their monies back.

Surprisingly the days passed quickly and Liam, Edmund, Mary and Megan found themselves beginning to repack their belongings for disembarkation in New York Harbour. But their journey was not without one more twist. On the morning of the eleventh day at sea the Duty Officer came down from the Bridge to make an announcement. The steerage travellers gathered around the kitchen area, with the Duty Officer standing on a raised platform. "I have some important news for some of you. I have the sad duty to inform you that the Purser attached to steerage duties has been found dead this morning. It is believed he has hanged himself. A total of $341 dollars three gold chains and a silver locket were also found in his cabin. It is believed when the captain ordered an internal search of the cabins the purser was found with the goods last evening and confined to quarters. Sadly he could not face the consequences and hanged himself in the night."Edmund immediately spoke. "I hope I can speak for all of us in saying how sad we are to hear of the Purser's death. How do you propose to distribute the money?"

"Sadly I expect there will not be sufficient to meet demand as we suspect he was not alone. Those who can prove what money they had will be first to be recompensed, the rest of the money will be equally divided among those with a claim. Gold chains and lockets will also need to show proof of ownership."A crowd of claimants began to gather, Mary also waited in line. Within the hour Mary returned to steerage with twelve dollars. Unfortunately she was unable to prove what had been taken and received a share of the remaining bounty. Edmund immediately got up and without saying much except a few mumbled remarks left for the Duty Officers Office. The Duty Officer recognised him on entry. "How can I help?"

"Call me Edmund"

"Fine Edmund, did you have items stolen, if so there is only a locket and one gold chain left."

"I've come about the locket," he answered casually.

"We have asked all claimants to describe the inside of the locket."

"If it's mine it will have a picture of an old lady with grey hair and wearing a silver broach on her right shoulder."

"That's correct Edmund. Who is this lady?" he said as he handed over the trinket.

"She's my mother."Edmund added gazing down at the small picture, "Was there a letter of Introduction to Dunwoody's with the Papal Seal attached, also found?"

"I'm afraid not, so far only money and jewellery has been found. We will search the cabin again but I doubt we will find anything. Was it important?"

"Only to my father, and to the priest." Edmund responded wondering why he felt so unconcerned. When he returned Liam and Mary were almost packed .With the ship due to be docking at 10am the following morning Edmund set to on his own packing but said little about the locket to Liam or Mary but mentioned the Captain thought the robberies were gang related. The night passed slowly but the following morning as dawn broke there was a mad scramble for the portholes to witness the passing of the Statue of Liberty as the ship entered New York Harbour and berthed by the Ellis Island docks. Chaos and excitement reigned as the realisation hit them that they had crossed the Atlantic. They marvelled at the majestic green-hued statue saying it was either bigger or smaller than they had thought. Friends hugged each other knowing that this may be the end of one dream and the beginning of another. As they moored up the sounding of fog horns began like some Offenbach opera echoing across the docks. Edmund looked at Mary reached out and held her hands. He trembled partly at the gentleness of her touch and partly at the sense of foreboding he had about living in the Five Points district. As the travellers turned grabbing their belongings to make the return journey up the steep flight of stairs to the middle deck and dry land , they glanced behind for one last look at their marine home. The gang planks were in place by the time they reached the middle decks. Streamers were floating down from the first class cabins. The ship's brass band playing "Dixie", started up in the first class lounge. Dancing started to break out. A flurry of people, travellers, seamen, porters, stall holders, stewards along with thieves, rapists, organised gangs surged on to the quay as their prey the newly arrived smiling entered the new world of good and evil. The four friends finally put their feet on the final gangplank, for one moment they all share the same thought and turned in unison to hug and kiss each other and thank God for their safe passage. Mary hugged Megan close and silently asked for God's forgiveness, but she knew it wasn't God's forgiveness she needed. Edmund and Liam were quick to return to the real world. "Let's be careful", they almost said together. They turned to the customs entry and proceeded to wait in line knowing they weren't on safe ground yet.

Chapter 3

St Cuthbert's Church, Cork: September 1924

'The Exodus'

The day of Matt's funeral seemed to come round quicker than anyone expected. When Owen arrived, the church yard was deserted. He had risen before dawn and had deliberately left early to avoid any discussion, knowing he needed to get through this on his own. Or so he thought. He had lived with Connor for a week now and learnt of the funeral arrangements indirectly. It already felt a strange day. Matt's death had numbed Owen's senses It was a neither here nor there, not cold, not warm, not dry, nor wet, bright but not bright, windless but not still. As he waited a low rising mist began to hover over the river and clog the early morning sunshine, engulfing the smoky dwarf cottages that backed onto the graveyard. The air tasted of burnt wood and a quiet numbness now settled over the church like a black cloak. Leaves fell silently. One. Two. One. Two. They flashed amber and gold, as they caught the intermittent fading rays of the sun. Owen nestled into the wall of the church trying to merge with its stony crags. His head ached through lack of sleep. He tried to remember when the whispering began. But now the whispered asides grew like a vengeance and fell like confetti around his ears making him feel a stranger in his own town. He loved his brother but now there were moments when he began to doubt his own thoughts. During the week at Connor's farm he had already noticed the reluctance of neighbours to talk, to move away or turn their backs on his coming. The worst was the rumour he had allowed his brother to die. He knew this was Joe's doing. Every night since Matt's death he had drunk the night away at Maguire's bar. He poured ridicule on Owen's testimony that he had crossed the Armagh Bridge before it was washed away. Connor had told him to forget it, that people would see it for what it was,' a man's grief'. But Owen did not believe him. Like the weather, Owen did not know what to do. He shuffled and fumbled needing to focus but his mind was engulfed with sadness. Matt! Matt! Tell them I did my best his head screamed. He wanted to cry and he wanted to beat the world. The falling leaves began to slowly cover his boots marking the passage of time. He kicked himself free and noticed out of the corner of his eye Connor arrive at the vestry door. He couldn't speak to Connor he was too grown up. Owen's younger sister was with him and something inside brightened. As soon as she saw Owen she ran across and hugged him around his waist. Tears began to brim on the edge of his eyes, but he held back. He desperately needed to be held, he needed his mother's arm around him but knew it would never come. He knelt down to kiss his sister's cheek and whispered "Don't forget me". She hugged him closer. Connor walked inconspicuously up to Owen and gave him a hard unyielding stare. "You got up early". Owen noted the edge to his voice but said nothing.

Before he could reply the church yard began to fill with people flowing in like the spring tide. Father Ryan appeared with Joe and his mother in the centre and moved as if floating on a raft of well wishers. Owen immediately released his sister and stood back. "Go back to your mother." She looked up. "Now", he muttered. She responded without words but she knew why and made her way into the church. Owen leaned his head back against the grey stone pillar and shut his eyes. His mouth hardened, aware that his heart was beating faster; his mother looked tired and distant still. Joe on the other hand looked like a man possessed. He seemed to walk on air using the arms of the passers-by like mobile crutches as he edged his way closer to the altar, his eyes firmly fixed on the coffin bearers. Owen took a sharp intake of breath as Matt's coffin came into view. Two bearers held his small body aloft and the crowd of onlookers grew quiet. Hats and heads bowed. He struggled to get his breath and murmured in anguish. "It's so small, It's so small." A handful of pigeons suddenly fluttered past flying in all directions and then regrouping and landing together as if tied by pieces of elastic bands on the heap of soil from the freshly dug grave. As the parishioners filed in behind Joe and his mother, Owen held back entering the church last. Connor watched Owen pick a pew and noted how the families turned away. He slid in beside Owen and whispered "You should sit with your mother".

"She doesn't want me."

"Don't be daft, support her."But Owen held his ground. Father Ryan looked in their direction and then began the service. Owen had missed the funeral wake held the night before giving absolution of the dead by the sprinkling of holy water on Matt's coffin. This was the moment for Matt's spirit to rejoin the living and wake from the dead. He began the service with the liturgy of the funeral mass with a penitent psalm. The words echoed around the church. Owen watched nervously. Connor put his hand on his shoulder. His eyes followed his mother's every movement. She stood still and heavy as if made of lead. Joe did not sing but murmured in a low crying voice; crying out each time Matt's name was mentioned by Father Ryan. Time seemed to pass painfully and slowly. As the service finished the coffin was lifted by the two bearers and steadied, to be borne to the freshly dug grave, while Joe and Mary moved to follow the coffin outside. Joe's murmurings and cries rose and fell with every stride the bearers took. His breathing grew heavy and coarse. Just as Father Ryan signalled for the coffin to be lowered to the earth Joe let out a piercing shriek and threw his arms around the coffin. "Please don't go, please don't go! Please stay. Please stay. Where will I go! Please don't go. Please! Please come back to me". He sobbed and sobbed for his heart was breaking. He sobbed the anguish of a father lost. Owen also cried, tears welled over his cheeks. Something in him made him know that in that moment he loved Matt but also that Joe loved Matt with all his heart. From that moment Owen felt differently about Joe but he never got the chance to tell him. Father Ryan, the curate and Doctor Lewis rushed forward consoling Joe and uncurling his arms from the coffin. Joe collapsed. Matt's coffin was laid to rest, Joe giving a muted, "No-oo,"as the soil was heaped into the grave to cover the coffin forever.

Owen threaded his way through the crowd leaving Connor to pay his respects to Mary and Joe. He found a shadowy corner under a Yew tree and sat to collect his thoughts. He was going over all the details of the night of the run in his head when a voice whispered, "Hello Owen". Owen turned to see Marion her eyes glistening, "I'm so sorry about Matt". She opened her arms and hugged him. Owen sank into her body and held tight and felt the tension begin to drain away. "Marion, it's good to see you." He almost kissed her. "Marion it's not true what they are saying."

"I know that", Marion replied, "and so do others."

"No one will believe me without evidence and that's lying at the bottom of the Irish Sea."

"People know you. But you must remember walking the Armagh Bridge in the middle of the night is a really unbelievable thing. Give people time."

"I haven't got time I have to find out what happened the night Matt died."Owen said changing the conversation. "What happened at Tincurry?"

"You mean you passed the gates of the Tincurry?" Marion's dark eyes widened.

"Yes," said Owen, "The gates were open and the lights were on, but no-one around."

"You were there I can't believe it" said Marion

"We were awakened at one o'clock in the morning and told to meet in the main hall. A large fire had been lit and we were told not to go near the windows. Father Ryan had joined us to say the grace for evening meal and then left. He was in discussion with the Warden for a while. The rumour was the Republicans were storing guns in the cellars."

"What cellars?"Owen glanced back to where Connor was speaking to Joe.

"It was always rumoured that before the war that guns had been secretly stored in some underground labyrinth from an outside entrance known only to a few families," Marion added, "at one point we heard lorries pull up in the main entrance".

"I saw nothing they must have gone by the time I arrived about three o'clock. So the Republicans were here and also at my place. Did the Tans call?"

"They arrived about three –thirty".

"So what of the three boys that absconded?"

"That was a hoax, no-one absconded it was cover for the gun - running to get the Black and Tans away from the House", Marion whispered for fear of being heard. "the excuse to the Tans was the boys were found hiding in the grounds."

"I could have been caught!" Owen said incredulously. "When I awoke the house was full of people. Some had gone, I counted fifteen cups for a meeting. Something to do with O'Leary's Farm and some maps pointing out underground pits for storage on our farm. Father Ryan is up to his neck in this. He must have known that the operation was underway."

"Careful Owen he's a powerful man."Marion's eyes flickered with alarm. "Have you spoken to your mother?"

"No, she won't see me" and he added morosely, "Joe wants me dead."

"Your ma is grieving although she seems to be carrying something more."

"What do you mean?"Owen raised his head.

"Something else is troubling her, something from the past maybe. I remember your ma being invincible. I always looked up to her."She smiled to herself remembering. Owen glanced back again towards Connor receiving a hostile gaze from Joe. He started ranting and gesturing. A single voice rang out from somewhere in the crowd of parishioners. "Owen Doyle please leave. You're not wanted here". Connor indicated with his head it was time to go and made his way back through the graveyard. Marion whispered, "Be brave" in his ear and kissed his cheek. "Meet me Sunday eight o' clock at the windmill". Owen distracted by the crowd was backing away but gave a single nod of his head and disappeared under the boughs of the

Yew tree. He met Connor on the south side of the church away from the village. He was waiting in the horse and trap "Get in Owen things are getting stirred up".

"Why! What have I done wrong!"

"Nothing lad but now's not the time to debate it. Owen clambered aboard."The horse moved off at a canter and Owen furtively glanced behind noting the growing distance between them and the agitated crowd massing at the edge of the graveyard. "Connor what's going on?"A Bentley three litre car appeared, accelerated and then, with a light touch of its horn and a wave of the driver's hand, it passed them. Connor ever vigilant noted the two heavy set men in the back seat. He immediately took the next left down a small dirt track overgrown with waist –high grass and wild bushes. Owen wondered what was going on. "A new way home Connor?" he said innocently.

"You could say that. Owen keep an eye on the lower road if a Bentley car follows us let me know."Owen stiffened realising something was up, something deadly. At first nothing entered the dirt track then suddenly coming at great speed the Bentley appeared, eating ground. "Connor", Owen uttered. His mouth taut. Connor without warning made a sharp turn right into a small wood, the trap weaving this way and that, in and out of trees, gathering speed with each crack of the whip. Owen rolled and lurched, clinging to the trap seat. The Bentley carried forward, unable to follow, on to the wider dirt track and now was running parallel with the trap about thirty yards away. Connor shot a look across and saw the window being wound down. He immediately pulled sharp right again heading deep into the wood shouting to Owen to get his head down. A shot rang out and hit a nearby tree. The trap continued to weave its way through the wood. The Bentley nearing with every second suddenly screeched to an abrupt halt and one of the occupants rolled out firing continuously in the direction of the trap. Two bullets pinged off the back of the trap carriage. A third tore past Owen's ear. The trap lurched and rolled and a sting of pain skittered down his side. The firing stopped and Owen lifting his head saw the thick set shooter re-enter the car and before he could close the door the Bentley was steaming down the dirt track to the main road."They 're gone" Owen mumbled trying to catch his breath.

"Which way?"

"Heading west towards O'Leary's Farm", Owen grunted attempting a smile, but almost on the verge of tears.

"They're trying to cut us off, it's not over. Hold on!"The trap made another sudden sideways movement pulling round a huge fallen tree and came to a stop under one of its arching boughs. Sweat poured off Connor's face. Owen sat as still as stone trying to comprehend what had just happened. "Are you alright?"

Owen nodded not sure if he had a voice. "It's not over Owen. We'll hold on here for a short while and then make our way back at dusk to the farm."

"Why are they after us?"Owen uttered clearing his throat.

"Not sure I hope Joe has not set the dogs on us". A million questions flooded Owen's mind wondering if it was Joe, did his mother know?

"Ahh" Owen cried out, his face twisted in pain, realising that a splinter of wood from the trap was sticking out of his thigh. Connor stepped from the trap and examined the wound. "It looks deep .Is it painful?"

"Not bad", said Owen wincing as Connor gently touched the end of the splinter. Connor went to the front of the trap to rummage in a small box. He returned with a small pair of pincers used for removing stones."This should do it. Have you got a handkerchief?"Owen produced a dirty grey piece of linen that hadn't been washed for days. "That'll do."Connor had a furtive look round satisfied they were quite hidden under the bough of the fallen oak. The horse chomped the grasses of the forest floor and apart from the occasional chink of the bridal all was quiet. Taking hold of the pincers ,Connor held Owen's thigh with his left hand and closed the mouth of the pincers over the splinter. "Hold on Owen". With a deft shrug of his body Connor removed the wooden splinter. It had penetrated about two inches and a flow of blood seeped to the surface. "Press hard."Connor whispered still looking around. We'll sort it out later, but should be good now."Owen wasn't worried about the wound. "Who were they Connor?"He said coldly. Connor eyed Owen as he wiped and replaced the pincers recognising that he meant business. "I can't say."

"Can't or want?

"I can't say but I will find out"

"Is Joe involved?"

"Probably, but I'm not sure." A silence fell between them. Connor for the first time in Owen's presence lit a cigarette. Owen was startled. Connor offered Owen a cigarette. Owen declined. Connor took a deep breath in and blew out gently stream of smoke. He spoke quietly and slowly. "Owen I need you to trust me. I'm going to ask you to take the trap back to my place. Go the long way round pass Clonmel Church and up the track to the Armagh Bridge. Owen listened without interruption. He knew that this would bring him out at the back of Connor's farm along a wooded lane hidden from the main road. "Half -way along you'll find a small outhouse, big enough to take the horse and trap. Aim to get there for dusk and I'll meet you there."He gave Owen a hard stare "We will sort this out". Owen held his breath. "Take care," Connor added ,turned on his heels striding up the wooded slope to a steep grassy bank. Within a few minutes Owen saw he had reached the top and watched him scan the horizon and roads and then break into a run, moving off towards the distant mountain peaks. Owen felt a sudden weight of tiredness overtake him. He tethered the horses rein to a lower branch and grabbing the small carriage rug settled with his back to the nearside wheel and closed his eyes.

Meanwhile Joe and Mary were locked in violent argument.

"You promised me no violence!" Joe replied with an almighty swing and caught Mary full in the face. "Don't tell me what to do!"Mary fell against the sink cupboard reeling from the blow, realising her mouth was bleeding. She wiped the blood away with her hand and without thinking, fired with anger and pain ripped into Joe again."You listen and listen good Joe Cahill. I've buried one son today if I bury another I find you and so help me God I'll cut your liver out. Now call off the dogs!" She was surprised by her response. Joe had continued to drink. His mind was a confusion of pain and frustration. "The republicans are nervous" he whimpered, "someone has been talking to the Tans. They are after blood."

"You know Owen and Connor have nothing to do with this. Oh why have I been so weak", she chastised herself.

"I don't know that Owen and Connor are clear. Do you believe Owen walked the Armagh Bridge? It's all cock. How did he get pass the

Garda and the Tans without being seen. They are in it up to their necks."

"Yes I do believe Owen. Maybe he's cleverer than you think."

"Believe what you like, I only hope he sorts it before the republicans sort it."

"Call the dogs off!" Mary screamed in desperation.

"Don't tell me what to do," and with that fell out of the door heading for Maguire's Bar.

Owen awoke with a start. He rubbed the sleep from his face and panicked. He looked around like a cornered fox about to be set on by a pack of hounds. Every things alright. Every things alright. He patted the horse and steadied the trap. His leg ached from stiffness as he climbed onto the carriage seat. It was about half an hour before dusk. Gently he eased the trap and headed out towards Clonmel. He was on red alert. Over the next half hour he saw and heard nothing and no-one. Partly relieved and yet still wondering where the Bentley was hiding. He knew if caught in the open he had no chance. As he entered the track leading up the valley he noticed a dark thick set man seated on the wall opposite the outhouse. He pulled up and edged into a small lilac bush covering the trap and horse from view. Fuck he thought. He tried to look further down the valley to the main road but he would expose his position if he moved closer. The man sat on the wall, lit a cigarette and then ducked down under an apple tree. From the road he couldn't be seen. Owen then had a bad feeling, Connor won't see him either. He'll walk straight into him. Fuck! Fuck! Fuck! Fear and tiredness gripped his being. Before he could think of what to do he saw Connor running and ducking his way down the hillside. The gunman would not see him till the last minute. Panic entered his mind. Think! Think! He had no options. No options he thought. With a crack of the whip he drove the trap forward at a fast gallop. The horse uttered a low whine. The gunman immediately lifted his head and crawled nearer the stone wall. Connor stopped in his tracks recognising the trap and wondered what the fuck was Owen doing. Until that is he caught sight of the arm raised, holding a gun at the arriving trap. Owen pulled to a halt. "Get out."

"Why what's wrong?"Owen tried to make time.

"Get the fuck out or die where you stand."Owen dismounted from the trap. "Now bring the trap in here," pointing at the outhouse. The gun man's face was half covered with a thick scarf. His eyes were unchanging. Connor threw himself on all fours and scrambled up to the remains of a stone wall. He edged his way forward till he came into earshot of the outhouse."Get over here! Move!" Owen felt a gun butt thud into his shoulder and he fell forward with his back to the gunman and his eyes to the open outhouse door. "Where's your friend?"

"He's long gone. Left me and headed towards Clonmel Church"

Owen suddenly spotted Connor and he knew he had to get the shooter to stand in the doorway of the byre. Unexpectedly the horse began to act up. He began to jump and buck. "Fucking hell sort this horse out"

"He needs feeding." Owen instinctively went to fetch the feeding bag but his movement was too quick for the shooter's liking. "Stop! Or" But before he could say I'll fire Connor held him in a powerful grip around his throat. In seconds he fell to the floor like a beached whale. "Connor!" Owen turned around in relief. His hands were shaking.

71

"Good lad"

"Is he dead?"

"No, but we will be if we don't get this sorted"

"Take his feet". Connor straightened up.

"Take him over to the apple tree."They dumped him solidly on the ground. They set the shooter upright against the tree and Connor completed tying a rope securely. Connor took his gun and put it in the tool box on the trap. They both for a moment, took a long moment to look around. No movement or cars .Nothing, they were in luck. They must have left the shooter as the only lookout. They would be back. Connor was deep in thought "Owen walk the horse and trap down to the farm and lock them in the far barn. Give the horse a good feed. They should be securely hidden there." Connor meantime checked the ropes again on the shooter. He then, picking up a shovel and sacks from the outhouse walked down to the field laid to potatoes and began to dig. Within what seemed minutes he was entering the farm door with a full sack, and left to fill another. Connor re-entered heavily laden with a second sack. Owen sat on a stool trying to imagine what happens next. "Owen we are in deep shit, the republicans think we've set them up. Something's happened to the guns. Once they find the shooter they'll search the farm. We need to stay here a good few days, we need them to think the farm is deserted."Owen took it all in. "How will we do that?"

"Well."Connor moved towards a trap door in the floor and on lifting revealed a set of deep wooden stairs. He led down and Owen followed. There was a large cavernous interior mainly built for the storage of potatoes and apples. Owen couldn't believe it. "My da dug it out the winter he returned from America with your da."Connor declared proudly. There was a good flow of air through and at one end, the air hole gave a good view of the road to the main drive. What made it perfect was the cleverly concealed back entrance on the   south   side. "We can hide out and sleep here for the next five days. Help me get the potatoes and bedding. Owen nodded with a small feeling of hope. Soon the cellar was ready to receive its new boarders. "What about food and drink"

"It won't be good but we won't starve. Each day we'll need to find a moment to go up the hillside to light a fire and eat. We'll cook some spare potatoes and eat them cold later. There's enough water and a few drams of potcheen will help us sleep." Connor returned up the stairs into the main hall of his farm closing the trap door. He quickly rearranged the furniture to cover the trap entrance. Making his way outside he locked the front farm door, knowing if he had put the metal bolt across the republicans would know they were still there. This way it would be assumed they had locked up and fled. He then turned to the south side of the house giving a furtive glance to the road. Once at the back entrance to the cellar he started to pull across some loose fallen branches and an old barrel to disguise the door. Then deftly stepping through the space created, he pulled the branches further over before locking the door. They were now safely locked in for the night or so they thought. Connor winked at Owen and chuckled to himself covering the sense of foreboding clouding his mind. He hoped they had prepared well, but any slip ups and they were caught like flies in a spider's web.

Time moved slowly. The evening moved on. Earlier they had done as planned and found a good vantage point, lit a small fire and cooked supper. Connor prepared colcannon, a mixture of cabbage potatoes and what was left of the bacon fried in butter and the remains of a boxty loaf. They kicked over the embers of the fire and returned to their safe cell, heading down in the evening light.

73

They talked and laughed a little, the effect of the putcheen, which helped to break the tension and ease the sleep. The night passed without incident. Owen was awakened by Connor at the first break of dawn light. Owen immediately checked out the main road. All was silent. Connor pulled a parcel wrapped in cloth from a corner of the cellar and set it on the sack of potatoes that now acted as the table. He carefully unwrapped, in immaculate condition, a Smith and Weston 38 calibre gun. "It belonged to my da." Connor proceeded to clean it further. He produced three boxes of cartridges and placed them on the makeshift table. "Can I hold it?" Owen, wide eyed and interested, muted. Connor adjusted the safety catch and handed him the weapon. Owen felt the weight, lifted it in the air and took sight. "Two hands, cup the bottom hand around the shaft. Good."

A rapid knock on the front door startled them. Connor had the good sense to immediately put his finger to his lips and gave a silent indication to move towards the air hole giving a view over the main road. No cars around. Probably someone on foot he thought. They sat stock still like frightened deer caught in a headlight. A second knock rattled the door. Connor's eyes jerked upwards. He retrieved the gun from Owen and proceeded to load it with great skill. A shrill voice barked. "Connor! Connor! It's Father Ryan." Silence fell. "Can we talk Connor?" Connor and Owen remained still and silent. Owen felt a strange feeling of heat on the back of his neck and pressed his palms together. A low droning sound began to rise from the road. Owen watched as two long shafts of white light glared across the potato meadow. Two figures bathed in light carrying the body of the unconscious shooter appeared from the right and bundled their load into the back of the waiting car. "Connor?" Father Ryan continued "If your there Connor I'll be at Maguire's Bar on Friday night, late on at ten. If you want to sort this out be there." Connor and Owen heard his feet retreating down the drive to the waiting car. Connor repeated his finger on his lips. The both held their breath and the car pulled away. Connor gingerly crept to the rear door and released the bolt without sound. He held his gun in his right hand. Without a word he opened the door some eight inches and squeezed out into the night. A soft breeze was blowing. Everything appeared normal. Nothing seemed out of place. Creeping forward he was able to see around the west side of the house and caught sight of the back of the car moving off in the distance. He quickly made his way up the slope to the outhouse to see that the shooter had gone. A thick band of navy blue rain was moving on a south westerly wind. He returned through the back entrance to where Owen waited in silence. Owen cleared his throat "What's father Ryan up to?"

"I'm not sure?" He paused. "I'm not sure if we can trust him?"Connor responded having already decided what he was going to do.

Owen awoke the following morning to find Connor had gone. He left a note with the simple words 'Stay put. I'll be back'. The day passed slowly. The rain had set in and a slow drizzle poured continuously. The patter of raindrops seemed to calm and quieten the day. Connor had left the gun resting on the sacks. Owen eyed it several times but managed to stave off the temptation to unwrap its linen cover. Suddenly Connor returned wet and flushed. Owen noted the blue circles under his eyes and wondered if his were the same. He produced four eggs and some thick rashers of gammon bacon. "Get the pan and let's eat". He responded almost light heartedly. Owen didn't need to be asked twice. They both emerged with the deftness of stalking tigers and made their way up to the cover of the wooded embankment .They positioned themselves so that any smoke from the fire would be carried away from the farmhouse. Within a few minutes the fire glowed and bacon sizzled. Connor broke three eggs into the pan. He gave the pan an angry shake.

"Tell me again what happened at Armagh Bridge." Owen was puzzled by the renewed interest but was too concerned with eating that he explained without fuss.

"When I got down past Buffers Cross windmill, I could see the bridge was very wet. A lot of water was cascading down and was well up on the rock pillars. I edged across and almost made it when my feet slipped under me. I thought I was a gonner when I realised my Da's walking stick had caught in a fissure in the rock. I pulled myself back onto the bridge and scrambled over. The walking stick wouldn't budge."

"So it was stuck on the far side of the river. Did you see the bridge collapse?"

"No".

"So it may have been swept into Chapman's pool." Connor paused for thought. "Time to go." Connor instructed, finishing his third cigarette. Owen nodded and moved off, down the wooded slope knowing that he had his own plans for the morning.

Even the early morning sunshine could not extinguish the macabre shadows that fell across the open courtyard of the Tincurry Workhouse. Marion awakened by the penetrating light, dressed and made her way down to the deserted kitchen. Stacks of unwashed and dirtied plates were piled in the two Belfast sinks. She turned on the hot water and watched it rise slowly. Her mind was full of uncertainties. It was now three years since she had lost her parents in a freak thunderstorm when a falling tree crushed their horse and carriage. Her life up to that point had been good. She had enjoyed life as a boarder with Owen at the Christian Brothers School. Her father was a doctor, colleague of Dr Lewis and great friends with Owen's father. She and Owen were good friends, perhaps better than good friends. Her life was thrown into confusion that summer's night and within weeks she found herself in poorer circumstances eventually being forced to take the hospitality of the Tincurry Workhouse. Despite her demise she had learnt to take care of herself. She was feisty and quick thinking and her skills and attitude had given her certain freedoms to come and go. She set to cleaning and restacking the dishes. An hour passed and she had finished without being disturbed by any inmates. She dried her hands and unlocked the scullery door. It was a warm day. She let the door fall shut behind her and made her way at a brisk pace across the open ground towards Clonmel church. She wondered if Owen would turn up or indeed if he was safe. She knew the Black and Tans were ruthless and had somehow caught on to the plan for storing guns across Cork County. The rumours about Owen were rife within Cambletown. Marion knew proof was needed of his innocence, but this was unlikely to be found. She hurried along furtively looking around. An unfamiliar car was parked up by the pharmacy. She halted for a moment turning left down Baldwin Street and came out in King's Square with its Georgian fronted houses. She slipped across unhindered until she saw a group of Protestant shop keepers stood chatting on the far side. Their eyes followed her and it rattled her nerves. She spotted an empty park bench on the grass verge and a voice inside said sit down for fucksake. She rested for a moment and a strange calm came over her. She collected her thoughts and rising slowly so as not to attract more interest she disappeared down a narrow passage way on the left. A rough shout dragged her attention away momentarily, but she walked on without responding. As she emerged, meadows opened up on both sides and the path began to rise steeply towards the Armagh Bridge, or what was left of it. Now free of prying eyes she increased her pace. The noise of the road died away as she climbed higher. She walked slightly off the beaten track, close to the tree line to avoid being seen.

She arrived at Buffer's Cross Windmill shortly before eight o'clock. She perched on a rocky crag, settled herself, before reaching into her bag for the apples she had collected before leaving. Suddenly a shadow fell across her legs and looking up saw another pair of eyes."Owen!" She rushed forward and embraced him and for the first time they kissed. The kiss lingered. Owen tasted the freshness of her breath and the fragrance of rose water filled his senses. Owen pulled her to him and she melted into his body, he could feel her breasts swell on his chest. He longed for it to go on but knew it could not. His kisses slowed and he pulled away gently. Their eyes met. He embraced her again needing her love and whispered "We need to talk." Marion kissed his cheek. Her sensuous eyes and parted lips invited his kiss but he gently lowered her down to the grassy bank."Owen it's good to see you," she said looking into his eyes. Owen tried to speak but was too overcome. She was so beautiful.

They didn't talk for what seemed an eternity but just held each other. Then, "Marion", Owen found his voice "Do you remember the night we camped here? We were about ten years old. My father; your father; me and you. Connor was ill and couldn't come. We had a makeshift shelter, but we slept under the stars. We talked and laughed for three whole nights. Do you remember my father talking of the four green fields?"

Marion nodded recalling the good time she had had with her father. Her words faltered so she nodded again. Owen continued "He talked about Ireland. He talked about the Irish being sprinkled across the earth like stars in the sky."

"Aye, I remember. The diaspora he called it".

78

"That's right diaspora", Owen blurted out suddenly recalling the words.

"Well Liam and your da were part of the diaspora for a short while. Your da asked us to name the four provinces of Leinster, Ulster, Munster and Connaught. I think I was the first to name the four." She teased.

"Do you remember that my father said the Irish word for province was 'cuige' which meant fifth and that he had found me the fifth green field?"

"Yes I do," Marion said forcefully. Then wondered where the conversation was going.

"What do you think he meant?"

She leaned across and kissed his cheek and her Irish red hair tickled his face. She could see he was troubled by the words." I don't know Owen," gently stoking his face as she spoke.

"Do you think he wanted me to become a priest?"

She waited what seemed an age trying to find an answer and not just a response. In the end it was a response. "I think your da was a very driven man who saw the troubles in our lives and wanted to change it. He was a true campaigner. He had high hopes for you. I don't know why he didn't become a priest. He would have made a fine priest. Everyone wonders how he got his money. I think Liam is the only one that knows. Liam also knows how the brotherhood works." Little did she know, that a woman also knew how he got his money and that she Marion would be the first to know.

"When is Liam due back from America?"

79

"In six months."

"Too bad," said Owen about to drop a bombshell.

"Why?"

"I shall be gone."

Marion sat bolt upright staring at Owen in disbelief.

"What do you mean you'll be gone", Marion interjected, half guessing the answer.

"I can't stay. I'm not wanted here. Besides, the Brotherhood think I betrayed them to the Black and Tans. They are out to kill me."Marion took a few deep breaths, her heart was racing.

Owen continued," Unless I can prove my innocence I'm finished. The longer I stay the more people I endanger. The only way I can protect them is to go. My life is elsewhere." The truth hit Marion full square in the face and sent shock waves through her body. She wanted him to stay but the price was too heavy.

"Where will you go?" Marion dreaded the question and the answer

"I don't know. I'll speak to Connor first."But he knew that he would not speak to Connor he had already decided and he knew he had but one option.

"Promise me you'll keep in touch," Marion almost pleaded. Owen nodded sensing it would comfort her but knew he could keep no promises. In his heart he longed to stay but he knew what he had to do.

"I have to go."Marion rose from the ground holding back the tears. "Of course you do," she said with masterful ease, "Of course you do."

Owen nodded. He leaned forward and kissed her on the cheek and turned away running down the crag before she could lift her eyes to return his kiss. She sank back on the grassy bank and watched him get smaller and smaller running down the valley floor. She suddenly realised she was holding something in her hand. She did not know how it got there but remembered his touch. She unfolded the paper and found a small locket. Inside, the petals of a blue flower with a yellow centre perfectly preserved met her eyes. She knew it instantly, it was a forget-me-not. Rising to her feet she placed her hands on the small pile of stones lying on the highest boulder. She took the top stone from the cairn and held it in her hand. Her life she felt was sometimes a series of events and this was just another event. It was almost that since her parents had died she had just existed. A feeling over which she had no control. Yet here she stood she thought on top of the world looking down on the village she was born in. In an instant she knew what she had to do and with a glimmer of hope she made deliberate steps down to the valley below.

Connor as usual had awoken early every morning and left to walk the mountains. Each day he had returned and evaded any prying eyes. No cars had been seen for the last two days. It appeared that the dogs had been called off. It did not stop Owen and Connor feeling nervous or going through what was now a well rehearsed security routine of looking for any movements around the farm. Friday morning came and Connor arose at first light. Owen was also awake but was in a sombre mood. They spoke very little. It was safer that way. He looked through the air hole to the main drive all was clear. Connor weaved his way through the narrow passage way and with a loose ambling gait made his way outside. The wind was keen and gusting and blew fresh air into the underground cell. Owen drank his tea impassively and watched Connor disappear from view. Owen had not noticed that Connor took a detour from his usual route, that morning, walking to O'Leary's farm and then down the path to Joe Cahill's farm as he now preferred to think of it. He hid behind two low growing gorse bushes and took a pair of old, well worn binoculars from his rucksack and scanned the outbuildings. All seemed quiet perhaps too quiet. He edged nearer and then squatted down behind a broken wall about fifty yards from the farm door. He crawled up to the pigsty and looked over its roof to see Mary and Joe pacing the room. He could hear raised voices. Connor moved with great stealth and glancing round knocked firmly on the farmhouse door. Joe appeared in an instance holding a gun, "What the fuck do you want?"

"I've come to talk. Put the gun down Joe." Mary for a few moments hesitated before stepping in front of Joe and embracing Connor."Connor it's good to see you."Joe withdrew his protest and sat awkwardly at the table while Mary made a brew.

"Have you called off the brotherhood?"Connor asked bluntly.

Mary shot a look at Joe. Joe answered cagily "They're holding their ground, but it's not over."

"What's the problem?"

"The problem is they think Owen betrayed them to the Black and Tans."

"You know that's not true!"

"Someone did."

"Why what's happened?"

"O'Leary is in gaol. Picked up by the Tans the night Matt died." Connor was visibly shocked.

"O'Leary was on borrowed time, he had a job to do but was incompetent. He left it too late to get that last delivery sorted."

"Well you tell it to the brotherhood."

"I will. Tell Father I'll be there tonight but I want safe passage." Connor asserted.

"I'll tell him but cannot guarantee it."

Mary butted in."Tell Owen I love him and I need to talk. There's things he should know."Joe looked angry and fumed under his breath. He stood looking out of the window.

Connor rose to go to the door, swigging the last mouthful of tea, "Mary it has been good to see you," and left. He swiftly turned up the valley and headed for the mountains. He had searched for days for Edmund's walking stick and now through elimination had only one place to look, Chapman's Pool. He headed upwards. It was gone dinner time when he reached Buffers Cross windmill and a herd of cows wandered across his path. The herdsman was nowhere to be seen. Connor moved down pass the mill and walked along the river's edge .He knew that much further down the river it would be deep enough to cross and get to Chapman's Pool. All the time he scanned the banks and under bushes where it had overgrown the river's edge. The weather was turning stormy and a dark bank of black cloud was gathering overhead. Connor realised he was running out of time. The light was fading. He increased his pace and a kind of panic set in desperately heaving overgrown bushes out of the way. Chapman's

Pool was not ready to give up its secrets. He systematically searched each area and then searched again. His mind began to fill with doubts. Was Owen telling the truth? It was almost unbelievable to cross the Armagh Bridge at night. The light had fallen to its lowest levels and exhausted Connor sat on a convenient boulder and felt despair overtake him. Sweat poured off his face and stung his eyes. .The humid evening was turning to rain and thunder. A flash of lightning suddenly illuminated the river. Something caught his eye. Then with great conviction like Arthur raising Excalibur he thrust his hand into the river and pulled out Edmund's walking stick. He sat back and laughed as rain covered his face. So Owen was telling the truth after all. And what a truth it was. All his tiredness suddenly left him and he made great speed back to Buffer's cross and home.

He arrived back at the farm at eight in the evening wanting to tell Owen first his news. Something made him slow down as he reached the back door entrance. Maybe it was too quiet but he couldn't be sure. The lights were not on as usual as he entered the cell with infinite silence. His eyes grew to the light and he realised Owen was not there. "Owen?" "Owen?"He found a small note on the makeshift table which he eagerly read .He sank to his knees and shouted, "No Owen! Why didn't you wait?" He immediately gathered his belongings and the walking stick and set off for Maguire's Bar.

Joe had reached Maguire's bar early that night. Mary had come with him but she was strangely different. Joe immediately started to drink, though Father Ryan on entering the public house told him what a fool he was being. They all sat around a large farmhouse table. Father Ryan at the head, Joe to his left, two Republicans to his right, O'Leary's son Sean, two more brotherhood followers, and Mary who sat behind and to the right. They sat and waited. Father Ryan led the discussion. The occasional couple out for an evening drink called in but soon took their leave and by ten o'clock the only table filled was theirs. The antique clock in the corner of the bar, the only piece of decent furniture in the bar, ominously struck ten o'clock. Tensions rose as the time ticked on .Then the door opened with a violent swing and Connor walked in. The republicans rose to their feet but before they could reach for weapons Connor threw the walking stick down on the table in front of Joe. Father Ryan looked left and right using his eyes to make the republicans return to their seats. They did so slowly. "Look at it Joe. Is it Edmund's?" Joe knew in an instant that it was but was reluctant to say. "Say it Joe, say it,"

"Yes alright it's Edmund's." Mary looked across to Connor.

"Owen crossed the Armagh Bridge trying to save his brother. It was an act of real courage more than most men would have tried. He didn't betray the movement. He never saw the Garda or the Black and Tans. He's completely innocent.

The listeners were stunned. Joe sat there looking down unable to meet Connor's gaze. Father Ryan said ", Have you told Owen the good news."

"No Father."

"Is there a reason?"

"Yes Father he's gone."

"Gone, gone where?" Mary looked horrified. Joe for the first time sat up.

"He's leaving Ireland for good. Right now he's in Belfast joining the British Army. Joe suddenly slammed his fists down on the table top, kicked it over and stormed out of the public house.

A quiet fell over the bar . Mary cried knowing Owen did not know how much she loved him . How much she had not told him and how much she wondered if she ever will.

Chapter 4

New arrivals ,both the unworldly and the unwitting to the Five Points, were always guaranteed a warm welcome. They were the uprooted, rich pickings and easily scammed by those in the know. The Lucania had moored up at the East Pier, to allow first and second class passengers to disembark. Edmund, Liam, Mary and Megan found themselves being redirected towards some waiting barges to be shipped to Ellis Island to the Immigration Centre. That's when the pangs of doubt hit Megan and Mary, instead of the euphoria and relief of arrival they both grasped the uncertainty of their futures. Mary had other dark secret concerns but tried not to let the despair drown her determination, but her knuckles gripping the guard rail were white. As she passed the second class cabin windows she caught a reflection of herself and instantly smiled to cover the inner turmoil. Mary looked at Liam" What's happening?"
"We," looking around at the other steerage travellers, "don't get to disembark until we have been through customs and a medical."The barge was quiet. The euphoria of arriving quickly dissipated and anxiety reigned. Many were tired, some were ill and others were fearful, having read the stories, they would be turned back. Megan having largely recovered from her illness began to worry she'd be left behind. Liam and Edmund had done their homework, they knew what to expect from the customs and also of the Five Points. Letters

home, newspaper cuttings, notes from friends and word of mouth from returnees had warned them of what was to come and offered smidgeons of light on how to survive.

It took two long hours before the foursome were processed and returned by barge to the quayside. They stood on the gang plank nervously waiting to disembark. The huge crowd that had gathered swayed to and fro like a spring tide. They eyed the travellers like wolves dividing the lambs from the ewes. Edmund looked around protectively and said, "Stay close," trying to cover his anxiety. He turned and blurted out again, "Don't get separated," as he gathered his carpet bag and his few belongings together. Megan held tight to Mary's hand and Liam braced himself for the hassle to come. He had positioned himself in front of Mary and Megan and Edmund slightly behind. They constantly exchanged glances, half-knowing what was to come, but being constantly surprised by what happened. Mary sensed the emotion rising in her fellow travellers, wanting to place their feet on American soil, but full of trepidation about where would they rest their heads that night. The quayside was a chaos of activity. Porters madly manoeuvred trunks and baggage piled high on four wheel trolleys, in and out, dutifully following the last of the first class cabin passengers off the dockside pathway. Children, orphans, waifs littering the dockside terrace, mingled with this procession of wealth holding their bowls, shouting, pleading, challenging, imploring with their eyes for a few small donations to buy their food for the day. Horses whined and shuffled around rocking the waiting carriages. The engines of the waiting Fords and

Chevrolets sprung to life, moving off with their well travelled occupants. The brass band struck up the Maple Leaf Rag just as the four travellers started to walk down the long gang plank to the quayside. The melody uplifted their spirits and they almost skipped along to its beat. As they touched American soil they lifted their heads striding forward like Christopher Columbus into this new land.

The travellers moved as one down the gangplank, clinging to their family groups, but as they streamed across the quayside wide spaces opened up between them and the two crowds, the waiting and the moving, merged together. Prying hands grabbed for bags and only the weak or ill could not fend them off. The foursome moved slowly, heads forward focusing on the quayside gates and the open space beyond. An Irish voice cried out in Gaelic, "Dia Dhuit! Hallow darling. Why aren't you the pretty one. Do they still make them in Ireland as lovely as you?"Mary half –turned to see a grey haired forty year old man with a wide grin and a red shirt. In his hand he held a stovepipe hat. His eyes raked across her body mentally feeling the firm young bosom and neckline. Mary shuffled and then carried on, but he maintained his pace and continued his patter. Edmund was too busy scanning and moving through the crowd that he failed to notice the extra baggage they had collected. He caught the tail-end of the discussion. "So maybe you need accommodation? Well Your luck's in."Mary was not to know that there was plenty of accommodation in the Five Points but very little of it was safe or fit for human habitation. Edmund smiled at the man, looked him up and down, and seeing his red shirt and stovepipe hat realised he was a Bowery Boy, an old Bowery Boy. The Bowery Boys were a feared, certainly by the Irish, hostile gang that controlled vast parts of Lower Manhattan. Over the years since the famine in Ireland their leaders had been killed and the gang had fallen from power. Edmund guessed the man was living off past glories, down on his luck, as the gang no longer existed. The man looked ill and hungry, months of starvation had heightened his cheekbones and widened his eyes and was no match for Edmund let alone Liam. But Edmund was still taking a chance. He leaned over, without dropping his pace, stepped between him and Mary, and spoke in Gaelic. "Dia dhuit. Hallo friend," looking him straight in the eyes. "Have you heard of Edmund Doyle?" The man caught off guard stopped the patter and shook his head. "Well be very afraid as he will tear your balls off if you don't move on now."The man immediately halted in his tracks and turned, doffed his stovepipe hat, only to glance, only once to see and remember his assailant. Liam realising what had happened drew Mary and Megan to the cover of four large bails of Egyptian cotton ready for loading onto a nearby tug for distribution. "He's a runner Mary. There is probably no accommodation. Keep a lookout for the hats, but the gang is long gone. Stay close" and smiled at Megan who was beginning to feel her vulnerability. They made their way through the dock gates and into Manhattan. The crowds began to disperse and melt into the streets and alleys. The foursome passed Coulthards Brewery, a dray and two large horses resting at the sidewalk waited for the drivers to appear.. Large wooden barrels filled the back of the dray. They moved on up Orange Street towards Lispenard Meadows, the main source of drinking water in Lower Manhattan. A billboard carrier offered a Square Deal to all Americans from their newly appointed president Theodore Roosevelt. Edmund, his eyes everywhere, constantly weighed up the industry, inns and taverns, thinking of the possibility of work, knowing they only had between them enough money for three weeks. His doubts as to what he would do about his priesthood continually surfaced like a dead body on a rising tide. Moreover he knew he was in a war zone, murders and rapes took place every day and night. To make it worse it was hard not to notice the Irish were not the flavour of the month. The anti-Irish, anti-Catholic feeling had reached fever point. The indigenous Anglo-Saxon Protestant white groups had become afraid of being overwhelmed by the influx of these poor immigrants. A poster on a door advertised 'The Six Social Sins' a forth coming lecture by the well known theologian Rauschenbusch. They walked on, after two miles reaching Collect Pond, a drained salt marsh in mid-town Manhattan. It was hard to avoid that every large space was filled by newly built Protestant churches and increased the feelings that this was not the Promised Land, and that milk and honey was off the menu. In times of change unlikely bed fellows occurred. The American industrialists, the Robber Barons offered to build these churches even though they supported the use of child labour. On every corner and every kerb, men in suits and bowler hats, sitting on their haunches, scouring newspapers for jobs and information. Change was rapid and violent. A paper carried the headlines that Suffragettes were breaking the windows in

Downing Street. A rickshaw pulled by a young Chinese man, full of Chinese lanterns, raised foul obscenities as it passed at speed. As the crowds thinned, Liam noticed a grocery store next to a liquor store on the corner of Orange and Anthony Street. He called to Edmund. Edmund and Mary decided to go and buy food for their supper later that evening. As they walked in Edmund could tell the shopkeeper had already made up his mind they were Irish. They had instantly realised on seeing the waiting crowds that they were wearing cheap and out of date clothing. This was the last thing they wanted, to be different. Others noticed as well. It was confirmed to Edmund when he asked to buy some bread and cheese. They exchanged greetings. The keeper inquired "Just off the boat?"

"We are sir," Edmund replied politely. The shopkeeper knew in an instant Edmund was a skilled man.

"Will you be wanting lodgings tonight?" the keeper replied with a slight accent.

Edmund paused for a moment, "Do you know of any available?"

"Is there many of you?"

"Just the two of us, and two more."

"And where are they?"

"Outside." pause, "Can I ask you, sir. Do you have lodgings?"

"I might have."

"Can we see?"

The shopkeeper continued to evade answering and continued to ask questions.

Edmund ran his hand over his thick crop of hair and down his neck. He wondered where the conversation was going, but didn't want to lose the possibility of some good accommodation by showing his anger. He smiled the way he always did when he was taking a risk, and asked again, "You do have some accommodation?"

The keeper, grey-haired but bright eyed, undid the apron he was wearing, and sensing the unease replied with yet another question."I can tell you are an educated man, we don't get many coming this way. Can you add a column of figures?"

"I can."Edmund replied.

"Will you add these for me?" and tossed Edmund a ledger with a line of figures. Edmund looked down the line and replied almost immediately "Sixty five dollars and forty two cents."

The shopkeeper almost gave a self –congratulatory smile, having teased out the vital information. Another question followed."Are you a book-keeper?" His secret was safe they had no idea what he planned. There was a silent pause before Edmund responded, "I can keep books but I have other skills." The shopkeeper only half-heard the answer, he was already getting his overcoat, while shouting to his wife, "Anya, just going out."Edmund picked up that her name was European. The grocery owner turned to Edmund, while smiling at Mary, and said "Shall we go?"Edmund looked towards the door, just as he was about to go, another question. "Don't you want these?" Edmund instantly turned, a frown almost crossed his face, when he realised the keeper was holding his cheese and bread. "Yes. How much?"

"Forty four cents", his wife Anya replied. Following the exchange of money and goods the shopkeeper led them out of Paradise Square towards Lispenard Meadows. They met Liam and Megan outside and the shopkeeper, Gunter, shook hands with them all. Gunter was a Dutch immigrant whose family had lived in the Five Points for ten years, his father having built the business. The smell of Banyards Slaughter House lingered in the air as they moved through a frenetic crowd. Life was fast and furious and at worst nasty and short. Suits and hats mingled with a surfeit of horses and carts, cars and bicycles. Every so often a scream or violent shouting would rise from the narrow alley ways. A barbers shop offered shaves for ten cents. A church warden gave away free coffee at the Bowery Mission Centre. Parcels, boxes and racks of newspapers peppered the edge of the road. A fire appliance doused the last remaining debris of H. L. Flynns Stables and coal yard having burnt down in the night. Squalid tenement buildings rose like black clouds blotting out the sun. These shoddy wooden structures had sprung up overnight in yards and back alleys to be rented out at exorbitant prices. In places brick tenements had replaced the flimsy wooden accommodation. Most were poorly sanitized and were cesspools of disease and prostitution. Even within the newly built very few rooms received direct sunlight, most were plagued with foul air and semi-darkness. In summer they became stifling saunas with most people sleeping if they could on the flat roofs. Tuberculosis was rife, the irony being that 'tubercle bacillus' is killed off in sunlight. Musty damp cellars were the other alternative, but most off the boat had merely exchanged one kind of steerage for another. Boarding houses abounded. Rising high to the east the Knickerbocker Hotel an awe-inspiring twenty-two storeys almost touched the sky. Liam and Edmund took up their positions as before one in front, one behind Mary and Megan, feeling the heightened interest they attracted as they moved through the narrow streets. People brushed and pushed past them knocking them off balance. Mary tightened her grip on Megan's arm. Glimpses into the boarding houses brought a mental shudder. How could anyone live in these vermin-infested hell-holes? Along the way they passed travellers new off the boat sitting, confused and gaunt, on walls and kerbs like cast out litter and garbage. Liam felt in himself a growing anger as he picked up NINA sign after NINA sign (No Irish Need Apply) on doors and windows and he began to doubt if he would ever find work. Suddenly he was distracted by two men locked in violent embrace, falling to the ground in front of them. A small crowd gathered instantly. Liam and Megan became separated on one side of the crowd. They drifted unaware of their separation, distracted and attracted by the violence of the struggle. Only Gunter realised the danger. He immediately dragged Edmund and Mary at the same time to the back of the crowd."Get your friends" and then added "Don't speak." Gunter knew the anger in the crowd could easily turn into Irish aggression. They were in an area of strong Protestant make-up and a mob of Protestant workmen had burnt down a Catholic church in the Irish Quarter only a week ago. Fear of the Papacy had become fear of the Irish. The five moved on quietly .As they moved out of the area into Orange Street Edmund looked back at the outpourings of human misery they had just witnessed and wondered by what irony fate had named it Paradise Square.

They headed up past the Chinese Theatre on Bowers Street, little knowing that this was not just a place of drama but the scene of several horrific murders. Banners advertising coming attractions were stretched across the street, engulfing the unlucky walker who failed to notice how low they were. Moving on at a pace they passed The Black Horse Tavern and Barney Flynn's Old Tree House Bar. Gunter halted for a moment while they collected together outside the Chinese Tuxedo Restaurant before moving on. By now they had walked a mile, for some it was one long gauntlet. Liam and Edmund made mental notes of the chances of work and the chances of death. Quite frankly they were everywhere. But his eyes were soon on a cluster of men in deep discussion. One of them looked up and from the snigger on his face recognised Edmund. Edmond recognised them, it was the group of Scandinavians he had irritated on the boat. The apparent leader doffed his peak cap and smiled menacingly. Edmund stared for a moment and then looked to move on. The Five Points was becoming their worst nightmare. They came to a sign hidden behind a yew tree, and for those in the know a moment of hope. It proclaimed the Tenth Ward. This was the New Israel, a place for Russian and East European Jews. Many had lived in Odessa in the Pale Settlement on the borders of eastern Russia. They had fled the pogroms, 'Juden verrecken-Death to the Jews', to find a better life in America. Edmund tried to collect his thoughts but was stunned by the sudden change from chaos to order. Sweat-shops were everywhere, steam irons hissed, needles clicked, laundries were on every street corner, shops and stalls offering Jewish fayre were in abundance. People were gracious. Edmund made the mental link between Gunter's wife being Eastern European, and Jewish. Gunter gestured to Edmund, "Not far now."

"Do you live here Gunter?" Perfect at not answering questions Gunter merely added, "I know the place well." Edmund beamed to himself for despite his evasive tactics he was beginning to like Gunter. Gunter walked on another hundred paces and stopped outside a thread-bare battered door. In fact it was two half doors both in poor condition. A sign declared First Floor Restaurant. A well-worn wooden staircase led upward. Two Jewish men passed them on the stairs exchanging greeting with Gunter but avoiding eye contact with Liam, Edmund, Mary and Megan. The treads on the stairs had worn to such a degree that it was only possible to get a purchase at the edges. Gunter stopped at a half painted door and taking keys from his overcoat he proceeded to unlock the door. The door opened on to a further set of stairs. Gunter gazed around as if checking that everything was in place and motioned, "It's up here. I hope you like what I have to offer."The stairs became narrower but at the top opened onto a large landing with three rooms off, two bedrooms and one main room. Each room had a sky light and the main room had a small window and door leading to a roof terrace. They all walked the rooms. Liam and Mary surveyed the room together. Megan and Edmund followed. They spoke in muted tones and eventually stood together on the roof terrace looking over the Five Points. Edmund found himself saying from here even the Five Points looks quite beautiful. Gunter could tell by their eyes they all liked the accommodation and like the good shopkeeper he sweetened the deal. "I'll get you two beds, a table, a cooker, and four chairs by this afternoon. Anything else you buy" and then added, "But I need a book-keeper. Wages are thirty dollars and rent is eight". The four looked at each other and almost as one they said "We'll take it." Gunter was over-joyed, he rushed forward shaking all by the hands. Edmund took Gunter to one side his mind full of small concerns and looking him full in the face asked, "Why are you doing this?"

"Doing what?" returned the question.

"Being so good to us?"

"It's simple. I have some vacant rooms. I need a bookkeeper, someone I can trust. I like your face, so for thirty dollars a week I get both problems solved"

He looked steadfastly at Edmond who nodded at the logic of his reasoning.

"See you sharp at seven –thirty. I will come for you," he added, waving a finger of good bye, as if to stifle any response, he turned on his heels and descended the stairs. As the door closed below the last shafts of sunlight brightened the room and Edmund thought things were looking up. But he was wrong. Within the hour the beds, table, cooker and chairs had arrived and the four ate their bread and cheese supper with coffee, their first meal under an American sky. Mary and Edmund stood for a while on the terrace overlooking the rooftops of the Five Points, watching the smoke rise and dwindle and the lights turn on and off. They held hands and kissed both knowing today had been a day of good fortune and they hoped it would last.

The Scandinavians had just finished their evening meal, all swilled down with large glasses of rough whiskey mixed with water. The remnants of a large newly caught fish rested on a dented metal platter with a heap of broken bread. Empty plates were strewn around the floor and some on the edge of the large central table. Small, piles of paper dollars and loose change, nickels and dimes, lay in neat constructed towers in the centre of the table. Around the table eight bodies sat and sitting at the head Stovepipe, a grey haired forty year old man in a red shirt. "So you think the cocky Irish bastard and his lovely ladies are holed up at the storekeepers place. You saw them enter?"He gave a hard unblinking stare at Hollow Legs, who stared back, swilling down a large gulp of whiskey, his fifth of the night giving rise to his reputation that he could drink anyone under the table. Hollow Legs grinned, "Yep all penned up for the night."
"Good work Legs". Hollow Legs grinned again, remembering the first time he saw the Irish man in the ticket office at Liverpool.
"Good. Good." Stovepipe muttered and looked around the group. He began to scoop the takings for the day into a large money casket and slid the chest into a cupboard with a cast iron door. "Tomorrow we'll watch and learn and then when we are ready we'll pay the Irish man and his lovely ladies a home visit, a house warming!" A ripple of hungry laughs flitted around the table."We sure w-w-will," said Stutter, the youngest member of the group. His eyes switched nervously from one face to another, looking for respect but none came. Several of the gang started to bunk down for the night and soon Stovepipe stood alone, looking into the night, and

looking eastwards, he murmured to himself, "So you'll tear my balls off, well be afraid Edmund Doyle."

Edmund awoke and looked around as the first rays of dawn filtered through the skylight spreading a hazy light across the room. He had never felt as rested as he did now, but an alarm bell suddenly went off in his head and a sense of panic and urgency overtook him, realising that Gunter was arriving in ten minutes. Liam sensed Edmund was awake and raised his head from his makeshift pillow. The room was freezing cold and there was no wood for the fire. Edmund had no sooner dressed when he heard heavy footsteps mount the stairs. A firm knock resounded across the room. Edmund unlocked the door and Gunter fresh and bright-eyed walked in. "Ready?" Gunter questioned. Edmund smiled to himself, another question flashed across his mind. "Of course, Gunter."

"Good let's go," pause, "Oh tell Liam to meet us back at the store at eleven, and bring Mary and Megan."Edmund relayed the message to Liam who had gone back to sleep. Without opening his eyes Liam nodded he understood. Edmund collected his coat and met Gunter on the stairs."What are your plans Gunter?" Edmund asked knowing he had plans of his own. He needed to make contact with the seminary but more importantly something had triggered a memory of a small shop he had seen in a narrow lay-by off a street near Gunter's store. If it was what he thought he was excited to find out. Gunter led the way and waited by the half panelled front door for Edmund to catch up. The street was a busy ,chaotic kaleidoscope of activity as they made their way to Gunter's store, both unaware they were being followed .Gunter was excited and talked incessantly, "I have big plans Edmund, very big plans." Edmund watched and nodded, keeping his powder dry. And then he saw down a track between Gunter's store and the Chinese Tuxedo Restaurant, sandwiched in between a row of smaller shops a red and white sign. The moment Edmund spotted the words Pari-Mutuel in the top corner of a white, one windowed shop front, he knew he was right. The speakeasy as some would call it was open early morning till late, serving coffee and refreshments, but more importantly was a betting shop. Wandering across to the betting parlour with its ever ready wireless commentary floating across the airwaves was to become a habit in his lunchtimes and early evening strolls. The pari-mutuel system meant the pay off odds were not set by the bookie but by the volume of betting by the whole public on a given horse on a given day. Public could mean ignorant bettors or legal gambling syndicates who could wager on behalf of a pool of people. It was a franchise, sponsored by big business and that meant big pay-offs. What interested Edmund even more was it operated as a bucket shop, which specialised in stocks and shares and allowed the small investor to bet on price fluctuations during market hours. Edmund was as thrilled to calculate the odds on horse racing as he was evaluating the price of wheat in five months time on the futures market. He knew if he was careful he had a chance to make money, lots of money, but he decided not to say anything until he knew the place was straight. Bucketeers, bucket shop owners were notorious for shady practice and could, by causing the price on ticker tape to momentarily move down wipe out a punter's margins, thereby taking all the profits. As long as you knew what you were doing you were unlikely to fall for such a scam. But did he really know what he was getting in to.

As Gunter and Edmund arrived at the store, the door opened and Anya his wife greeted them. Gunter touched the Jewish mazuzah on entering the store and Edmund could now see the strong Jewish features and the underlying east European accent. He began to show Edmund every aspect of their grocery and chandlers business. Gunter's father, a Latvian immigrant, had been a small business owner in Amsterdam and later in Atlanta, before working as an agent for a Boston shoe manufacturer and eventually settling in New York where he was able to buy the shop outright. Sales had flourished and the store was well stocked. The mixture of smells of rosin, turpentine, tar, pitch, linseed oil whale oil and leather permeated the whole store. At the back, an array of tools hatchets, axes, hammers, caulking irons, hand pumps and marlinspikes hung from the rafters. Brooms and mops, fashioned leather goods and wrapping papers covered every inch of the wall leading into the kitchen. Even by eight o'clock the store was brimming with people. In the course of the morning Gunter had taken Edmund through their accounts, invoicing systems and how to calculate the day's takings. It was clear even at this early stage the store had a good turn-over of sixty seven thousand dollars. It was also apparent that the ships chandlery business from the Hudson River was central to the existence of the store. Edmund was deep in thought when Liam Mary and Megan arrived. Gunter greeted them and led them to a room at the back of the store, where he offered them coffee and flapjacks. As breakfast had not been inspiring, the three ate well and soon another plate of flapjacks replenished the first. Anya took Mary and Megan off to a small store of ladies clothes and toiletries and much laughter and discussion continued into the afternoon. Gunter meanwhile had offered Liam work as a part-time stockman, which he gladly accepted. He showed him around two vast barns at the back of the store, containing boxes of spare stock, some which was damp. He left Liam to resort the damp stock.

At lunch Edmund couldn't wait to wander across to the speakeasy. A surly looking, overweight Chinese wearing a grey tunic barred his entrance. "What your bisness, my friend", he said placing a gentle hand on Edmund's chest.

"A cup of coffee and a horse to ride."

"You're new?"

"That's right." The doorman held Edmund for a few minutes without saying a word and then suddenly relented and said, "O.K. friend you may go in," and with that gracefully opened the door with his left hand. A ceiling fan whirred above Edmund's head sending a funnel of hot air and smoke around the room. The place was surprisingly packed with many men standing shoulder to shoulder along the walls, with an open space in the middle of the room. At the far end of the room, standing behind a well made wooden counter, stood a woman with shoulder length silver-hair. She was well dressed and in conversation with two men. She had noted Edmund's entrance while still continuing to serve the paper betting tickets to the two men. Despite the movement of air the room was hot and condensation streaked the windows across the back terrace of the shop. As Edmund got nearer she lowered her voice and the two men chuckled. He bit his lip thinking she had made a derogatory comment about Irish Catholics. He was surprised to see that when she spoke she was also Irish. "Dia Dhuit."She spoke in the same lowered voice. Edmund replied equally quietly. She asked a few questions about was he long off the boat, about lodgings and work. Edmund found himself acting like Gunter being evasive and asking questions, mainly because a muted silence had crept into the room.

"Do you want to place a bet?"

"Not yet but wouldn't mind a coffee."

"Coffee's free, bets cost yer."

The coffee arrived in seconds, bitter and very hot, having been on the boil all day.

"Have you any form sheets for the next race."

The silver-haired teller handed him a list of horses and riders and racing form. Edmund studied it hard. He knew form well and understood about physical condition and pedigree. He could judge horses that well especially if he could see them in the flesh. His father had taught him well. "Once a horse has shown its form the next most important aspect is personality, has it got the right attitude," he used to say. Edmund began to ask another question, but the telephone rang. She picked it up and turned away facing the large speakers from which emanated the commentary on the ongoing race. As she finished the call, Edmund smiled and asked "How does the stocks and shares work."Her eyes quizzed him quickly.

"You do stocks and shares?"

"Why is there a problem?"

"No! No! You surprise me that's all I thought you were a horses man." She handed him an explanatory note of stocks and shares terms and conditions. He took in the detail before responding. "A bit of both." He added looking up.

"A bit of both. What?"

"A bit of stocks and shares and a bit of the horses. For instance the horse that will win the next race is Middleground."

"Really! Clairvoyant are yer."

Edmund laughed. "Wish I was. See you tomorrow."

The silver-haired ticket seller smiled and Edmund turned to leave the shop. As he walked through the door the commentary on the overhead airwaves declared, "...and Middleground wins its maiden race by two lengths." As he returned Gunter greeted him at the door realising where he had been but said nothing. The afternoon passed quickly and Liam and Edmund closed the store and the four set out for their lodgings.

Darkness had fallen. The wind had turned colder and as the last warmth of autumn had faded, the moist smell of snow lingered in the air. The foursome picked their way slowly through the narrow side streets and entered the Bowery district of New York city, often coming across groups of men huddled in shop doorways or bedded down on street benches. Many were alcoholics, without the money to pay the rent, only to buy the bottle clutched in their sleeping hands. Many would die of hypothermia in the coming winter. Homelessness was another pandemic to hit New York.

Orphan asylums for Jewish, Catholic and Protestant children grew like bindweed across the city. A dark underpass lay ahead. The four stayed close. Liam carried a bundle of logs for the night's fire on his shoulders. A train had crossed the tracks above deafening all conversation. As they entered Edmund caught a tiny flash of light at the far end of the underpass. Even in the dim lighting Edmund could see a small man with his head directly interposed between the gas light and the underpass support wall, so that his face was in complete darkness. The four moved into the dark passage, Liam led the way. The early flakes of winter snow speckled the air, falling and disappearing in the warmth of the gas lamp. The movement of shadows made Liam slow his pace. His eyes searched the darkness. Something moved and he readied himself for trouble, as they passed the gas lamp, but whoever it was had gone. Liam could see the footsteps, in the thickening snow, of two men leading off into the distance. He kept his council and held his breath until the next time.

As the months passed Gunter and Edmund developed a close friendship. It was stronger than friendship, there was something special that drew Edmund and Gunter together. Both knew about hard, hard work. Both were stubborn enough to take on impossible odds. Both knew what it was like to be hunted and beaten and rise again, but more than this, in a world where the rules were continually broken, they found they could trust each other. And both in their secret moments thanked their lucky stars.Edmund had suggested several improvements to the chandlery trade, offering moored up ships a full service and a rebate for repeat business. Orders began to roll in. Even more rapid sales came from extending the range of women's clothes. Edmund had noticed how Megan's eyes feasted on the fashionable clothes in the Ladies World Magazine featuring the season's new dresses, resting on the counter. She longed to try them on but barely had the means to live each day. In an innocent conversation sometime afterwards with Mary about increasing the range of cottons, silks and satins, she mentioned she could make her own dresses .Gunter seizing the opportunity agreed to a trial run making replica dresses, to customer requirements. It was an inspired idea and Mary with Megan's help had weeks of work flooding in. It was also hard not to notice that Edmund was now beginning to make money on the horses, but more importantly taking substantial sums on the stocks and shares day trading prices. Doreen, the silver-haired manager, originally from Derry, had watched the steady run of payouts and wondered if it was the luck of the Irish or a clever scam of insider-dealing. At each subsequent meeting with Edmund, Gunter began slowly to reveal his secrets.

Snow fell incessantly in the few weeks leading up to Christmas. As night fell, a bitter wind would roll off the Hudson River icing the windows by morning. Gunter with Liam's help had seen to it that ample supplies of wood and coal arrived at the rooms. The single wood-burning stove radiated heat throughout, though Mary complained the washroom always seemed cold. Mary and Megan had fixed up a set of curtains made from old blankets across the door to seal out the draughts. Christmas fever was growing. Hot chestnut hawkers had sprung up everywhere. Adverts in the Gaelic American newspaper announced a grand Christmas fayre in Madison Square Garden's and a Christmas jamboree in Celtic Park, Long Island City. Mark Twain, was the honoured guest of the Plieades Club at the Brevoort Hotel. At the end of November, shortly after Thanksgiving the four had watched the Mayor of New York City switch on the Christmas tree lights in Times Square. Horse-drawn drays, piled high with cut trees, circled the city day and night. Megan and Mary made embroidered tree decorations that sold well. Macy's Department store promised to stay open until midnight on Christmas Eve. The New York Times proclaimed that J.P.Morgan had rewarded ten clerks with $5000 gold certificates. Oklahoma would celebrate Christmas as the forty-sixth state. Business was booming the goose was getting fat. The stock market was beginning to boom. The four-`some were beginning to find their feet, but the tranquillity wouldn't last. Nothing ever does.

One night as Gunter and Edmund settled to talk about the day's profits, he abruptly blurted out, "You have gathered by now we are Jewish."He handed Edmund a small glass of whiskey, Irish whiskey. Edmund nodded and sipped the malt knowing this was quite a revelation to make.

"My father was a shoe maker, but he moved a lot. As a child he lived in Odessa in the Pale Settlement, the only place in Russia that Jews could legally settle. But life was hard, very hard. He used what money he had saved to travel to Amsterdam, where I was born, to set up a shoe shop, but too many pogroms. So like a good Jew he moved again to Boston and then to here or New Amsterdam, as he would call it. As children we learnt

108

not to speak Yiddish in the open. We acquired several languages because of this. Anya is better than me and speaks five languages. We learnt how to make money and how to play the stock markets." He grinned and laughed out loud as if embarrassed. Edmund half laughed in return when Gunter continued. "But" he said I've never seen anyone as good as you Edmund. I wondered if we could share our thoughts and set up a fund to play the markets.

"Are you sure?" Edmund looked up, "after all there are no guarantees".

"We both know there are no guarantees in life, only risks". Gunter laughed again. Edmund wondered if the malt made him giddy. Gunter added "You know for someone who has come all this way to be a priest God gave you an amazing talent." Edmund winced inside knowing he still had unfinished business with God and didn't know who would be the winner. Three weeks had passed since Edmund in the early hours of one morning had written to the Rector Most Reverend John Levine, at the Arch Diocese of New York recounting the loss of the introductory letter. When it finally arrived a few days later, a letter bearing the College seal was left at Gunter's store. Edmund turned the letter over and over, placing it down on the table, making coffee, returning to touch but not open. He dreaded the response either way, your place is available or not available, and didn't know what to do. In the end Mary offered to open it and he consented. She opened it and read for a few moments.

"Well," said Edmund impatiently.

"The Rector Most Reverend John Levine is offering you an interview to discuss your situation." Edmund took the letter and read for himself. He placed it down on the table. The room felt warm but things were about to get a lot hotter before he would have to face the breath of his God.

The first body blow came, in the week before Christmas, one wintry night after Evensong. The church of St Bernadettes, stood at the top of a long, constricted lane opposite a deserted, mostly disused Neo-Georgian fronted building. Close by was a windowless, fronted structure used as a hall and training ground for Kildare Men's B&S Association. Snow made the walk up to the church difficult but a throng of parishioners had gathered to sing carols around the Christmas tree erected near the altar. Liam had left early having promised the tenants of the other rooms he would finish retreading the worn staircase, with plywood Gunter had supplied, before Christmas Day. Liam had carried the sheets of ply earlier in the day to the rooms, and began to set to on cutting and screwing the pieces in place once he arrived. The first he heard of it was the noisy flurry of fast moving steps coming up behind him. He instantly turned but was struck across the bridge of his nose with a wooden club. Dazed but still conscious, he rested on one knee to face his assailants. Three men, faces masked and wearing peaked caps barred his way. He knew instantly his nose was broken. His eyes felt tight and watered, his breathing was hard and laboured. He looked around for some protection and ripped up a piece of plywood still half-screwed to the stairs. The attack when it came was furious and brutal and despite his efforts, Liam was overpowered. The tallest of the three men grabbed Liam by the throat and screamed in his ear, "Tell Edmund

110

Doyle we want some of his earnings. Two thousand dollars, a little early Christmas present. Have it ready for collection by Wednesday. We'll be back." Liam, through blooded teeth told him to, "Fuck off", to which he received another blow to the face which sent excruciating pains across his eyes. Liam made a mental note of the red shirt and medallion hanging around his attacker's neck, before passing out. An hour later Edmund, Megan and Mary made their way back to the rooms.

"Tonight reminded me of Ireland, the choir is really coming on", Mary mused.

"I'm glad you enjoyed it," whispered Edmund still humming in his head the last strains of "O' Come all ye faithful." He felt for the first time since leaving Ireland that he was beginning to belong. As they neared the rooms, Megan suddenly screamed, "Oh my God! Oh God have mercy!" She started to run and turned, half – running backwards and screaming, "Edmund quick Liam's badly hurt." The three entered the hall without thinking and gently lifted Liam on to his side. The commotion had drawn attention and residents quickly brought hot water. Mary took over wiping Liam face and the blood from his cheeks. Still badly dazed Liam opened his eyes, his memory flooded back. He looked at Edmund, "It's the Scandinavians they want two thousand dollars by Wednesday.

"Don't worry old chum, let's get you in a bed for the night and think on it."

Edmund was in awe of Mary as she handled the cleaning of the blood from Liam's face which was now swelling around his nose. He had lifted Liam on to his shoulder and all but carried him as a dead weight up the stairs. Liam groaned infrequently but began to feel the effects of concussion overtake his body. He slumped on to the bed and its softness engulfed him. The last words he heard from Mary were, "Your nose is broken, and you'll have two shiners by morning." He remembered thinking it's a long time since `he had two shiners. Liam didn't hear the sound of muffled feet and voices that entered the room. Gunter appeared at the door with a man in a grey coat and small black bag. The bag was worn and well used but of a distinctive style and made of fine leather. Edmund rose to greet him and Gunter responded, extending his hand towards the stranger, "Meet my friend Mikhail", and added, "he's a doctor."

"How did you know", said Megan

"News travels fast, bad news even faster".

Liam though barely conscious did not feel the gentle examination that Mikhail administered. He looked at Mary, for some unknown reason, and explained in a strong Eastern European accent, "No bones broken apart from the nose, which will be painful for a week, but he'll have black eyes for Hanukkah. Take this for the pain," and gave Mary a small bottle of laudanum. "Use it sparingly it's addictive." Gunter nodded, pleased with the diagnosis, knowing his master builder would soon return to work. He turned to Edmund and asked "What happened?"

In a quiet voice Edmund explained, "The Scandinavians want $2000 by Wednesday," and moved to place another log in the stove fire. Mary had succeeded in giving Liam his first dose of medication and he was now in a deep sleep. "A good rest and a hot bath will have him back on his feet," Gunter said optimistically.

"A bath?"

"Don't worry I'll bring one. We need to talk," said Gunter who turned and left, his final remarks always final. An uneasy night followed. Edmund bedded down on the floor arose at five o'clock, the cold of the night penetrated the wooden floor and disturbed his sleep. It gave him time to think on what could be done and a plan began to form in his mind, but events would turn again before he could put it into action. By the time the metal bath arrived, Edmund had a roaring fire going and a pail of hot water already steaming. Liam eventually woke the swelling having subsided a little and his breathing was a lot easier. The warmth of the bath soothed the obvious bruises on his arms and back and he could feel his strength returning. Time seemed to hang in the air after the assault on Liam. The most important thing was for Liam to get better, but in every waking moment he seemed to fixate on how to deal with the Scandinavians. Gunter returned and beckoned Edmund onto the roof terrace the following morning with one question on his mind he urged, "You're not going to give them the $2000 are you?"

"No. They'll only want more. But what can I do? Liam is in no state to help. Between us we could sort it out, but he's not ready," whispered Edmund, sat on the stool deep in thought. Gunter offered to help but Edmund didn't want to escalate the situation, not just yet. He knew for the moment his only chance was to bluff it out, to gain time, but in the back of his mind he knew he may have to give up his hard earned cash. The days passed and Wednesday morning arrived. Liam pretended he was better and they could sort it, but Edmund knew he wasn't ready. Mary and Megan offered to help but Edmund knew they could all get seriously hurt if it went wrong. "I can't let them get hurt," said Edmund.

Gunter agreed, "You," and then corrected himself," We have no options."Edmund paced the room, hoping for a way out, little knowing that a window was about to open for him or was it a trapdoor. A breeze was blowing a thickening cover of cloud as darkness fell over Manhattan and Gunter's store. Barring a small light, Edmund and Gunter sat in semi-darkness waiting for Liam's assailants to make themselves known. Both fiddled around in their chairs as they waited and waited. They both didn't like waiting. They liked to be in control and felt they were like flies on a fishing rod waiting for a catch, but knowing they were the bait. Just as the last throes of light were disappearing, and just when Gunter and Edmund thought that no-one was going to show the door burst open and in walked three men. "Stay where you are gentlemen," the leading male dressed in a long coat, belted at the waist, asserted in a strong Irish accent. Edmund had half-risen, but settled back on to his chair. The other two males took up positions across the room, bolting the door, lowering the blind and checking for any hired protection. Once secure the lead male continued. "Gentlemen let me introduce myself, my name is Sean Kenny." Edmund's mind was racing. He knew the name, but it was a name from the past. He must bluff it out until he knew more. He reached forward for his half-empty coffee cup and swallowed a mouthful. "How can we help you?" Gunter asked the first question as usual.

Kenny almost ignored the question and focused on Edmund, "It's not so much how you can help us but how I can help you."

"Suppose you explain", Edmund added without looking up.

"Ah, Mr Doyle, it's a pleasure to meet you. It's a pleasure to meet the Campaigner." Edmund looked up, he was taken aback that he knew his personal details but although he tried not to show it on his face he had already given it away.

"Ah yes Mr Doyle you are surprised about what I know. Well I know you were badly beaten by the Black and Tans when you challenged the Kingston Estate over the Land Act."

Edmund tried to remain still, he was on the receiving end and smiling, he stood up and abruptly said, "Can we cut the small talk and the history lesson and get down to what you want of us?"

"Well said," Sean responded, clapping his hands, "My understanding you two lovelies are sitting here in the dark waiting for Stovepipe Red to come to relieve you of two thousand dollars. Well I am here to tell you he's not coming." Edmund and Gunter glanced at each other realising they had just got out of something simple into something more complex. Some would have said they had just fallen out of the frying pan into the fire. The realisation that the threat of the Scandinavians had just been eliminated suddenly jolted a memory in Edmund's mind. "Sean Kenny?" he muttered to himself, and then he remembered. "Sean Kenny from Kildare, Deputy Controller of Sinn Fein, wanted in relation to the killing of three Protestants in Ulster. Edmund was careful not to say murder.

"What a good memory, go to the top of the class. Surely a good Catholic boy is not worried about the death of a few Protestants." Edmund said nothing. Kenny continued. "Mr Doyle you are a good Irish man and like all good Irish men you want a free Ireland. That's what you're fighting for and I'm doing the same. We both belong to the same Brotherhood. The Brotherhood needs money for guns. It has not gone unnoticed that you have a gift for making money on the stock market. We at Clan na Gael."

"Clan na Gael!" Edmund interrupted. "You're working with Clan Na Gael".

"We at Clan na Gael", Kenny continued," want to sub you for $3000 dollars to invest in the stock market and by next May I expect to receive $15000 dollars from you. In return we will ensure the Scandinavians don't come calling." Kenny paused. "Think about it Doyle, you're doing the thing that comes natural to you. Any money you make over the fifteen thousand dollars is yours to keep. I will take the money to Ireland in June."

Edmund felt frustrated and angry but resisted the urge to do something rash. As he calmed he could see an escape route materialising. Gunter also surmised it gave them time to figure a way out. Edmund felt the guilty pangs of excitement at the challenge it presented, but had to know the answer to what happened if they failed.

Kenny's reply was short and sweet, "Don't even think about it, you're making money so why would you fail."

Edmund declined to answer, knowing there was nothing he could say. He looked at Gunter who nodded

116

reassuringly. He could see he was saying go with it, we can do it. He almost believed it. At the back of his mind a siren called out. How would all this go down with the College. He was due to meet the Holy Father in two days and what would he say. Kenny's cold eyes stared unfeelingly at Edmund, "There's no need for an answer as you have no options. So this is where we are. I'll be back in three days just before Christmas day. Think of me as one of the Three Wise Men, the one carrying gold. From that moment on you owe the Brotherhood fifteen thousand dollars –to be ready for collection at the end of May."

Edmund nodded affirming the deal but added, "Once the fifteen thousand is paid I owe you and the Brotherhood nothing."

"You owe me nothing, Mr Doyle, if you owe anything it is to Ireland." By now the door was opened and the three left and everything seemed to return to normal. Gunter broke the silence, "You seemed to know Kenny?"

"I know of him, but Liam will remember him I'm sure of that."The two knew what they had to do but Edmund's thoughts were on what he was going to say to the Holy Father in two days time. The door opened behind them and Mary entered having seen Kenny leave. Megan had remained with Liam. Edmund quickly filled in Mary on what had happened.

"Can we trust this Kenny?"

"Maybe, I'll know better once I've spoken to Liam.

Chapter 5

"March 1939, Jaffa, Palestine"

'' 'And it came to pass

Fourteen years had tumbled by, almost without Owen knowing, until a letter from Marion came out of the blue, breaking news that Joe had been found face down in a road side ditch with a bullet in his head. His mind jumped for a moment as his eyes trailed across her perfectly formed handwriting. He was still working out, what had shocked him the most; Joe's violent death; the passage of time; or the thought of Marion. He noticed in the top corner she had written Mtarfa H. Valetta, Malta. In an instant he had made his mind up what he would do.
"Bad news Sergeant?"
"What makes you think that?"Owen replied turning his attention to the Warrant Officer Jim McCabe stood by him.
"You looked thoughtful".
"My stepfather has died."Owen winced inside as he said it, much as he didn't want Joe dead, he'd had no love for him while he was alive.
"Oh sorry. Close was he?"
"Only for a moment." Owen murmured coldly, and an image of Joe at Matt's funeral came to mind. "Jim, I may need some leave? How's it looking? I need to get to Malta. I need to get to Valetta"

"Not good. If you are going to go; go now. Two days at most. The Arab leaders are getting stirred up again over the Israelis settling in Palestinian towns. Worse, things are not looking good in Europe." The recent increase in Jewish immigration and land acquisition, the growing power of the Hajj Amin Al Husayni, frustration with European rule had begun to radicalise increasing numbers of Palestinian Arabs. Something was about to blow, it needed only a small incident to light an inferno. Two years earlier an Arab attack on a Jewish bus led to a series of incidents that escalated into a major Palestinian rebellion. Owen pondered where the time had gone. After a spell at Caterham as raw recruits they were formed into a squad and subjected to the tender mercies of a corporal drill instructor and platoon sergeant. After Caterham he was sent to join the First Battalion Manchester Regiment stationed in Cologne as part of the Rhine Garrison on the Rhine. At least in Germany he was free of any Irish connections. Memories did however run deep and he remembered the whispers about the three young musicians murdered by republicans in County Cork, or worst still the ambush in West Cork of a motor lorry by one hundred and fifty Irish rebels, killing a British Captain, only served to breed distrust of any southern Irish newcomer. He laughed to himself realizing that even though it seemed a short time he had actually come along way. He had learnt to keep his head down and lived through the idle chatter, making his own mark and earning unstinting acceptance. The army had given him a new rhythm in life, a rhythm he had not found in Ireland. The fourteen years were full and passed quickly. He had crossed and re-crossed the seas of the world. At one time he was stationed in Bermuda, and latterly in Egypt, Palestine and the Holy Land. The English, he had been told from an early age, have a talent for destruction and sticking their nose in other people's business, and yet he had been confounded by their talent for nation building. He wondered if he should have done more to bridge the gap between himself and his mother. For a moment he thought of Matt and wondered if he had been quicker and brought the doctor would he ever have joined the British Army. It was something he wondered about every day. What would his father have said? And yet how could he have stayed. Matt was dead. The Republicans were out for his blood. How could he write to his mother or Marion? They had their informers they would be quick to take their revenge on his family and friends. He wondered why Connor had made no contact all these years. He had no real idea how things had been resolved. Perhaps writing was not Connor's strong point. What state would his mother be in now Joe was gone? She had lost three people in her life, perhaps four. In his time away she had written a single letter which arrived at the Caterham Barracks four weeks after he left Ireland. It was the only thing, apart from his rosary, he carried everywhere with him. He knew it by heart.

"Dearest Owen, my dearest son. You have taken the long Irish path of leaving Ireland. I hope you will return to me before I die. We have had a lifetime to talk to each other, but so many events have carried us apart. There is much to tell and much that your father wanted me to say. Please don't leave it too late. But if fate and God is

against me know that I loved you with all my heart. May the road home rise to meet you. God speed.
Your loving mother.

Two armored jeeps screeching to a dead stop outside the Administration block broke his thoughts. A glance outside told him they were the Special night Squad, a British and Jewish counter insurgency group , set up to defend the Iraq Petroleum Company pipeline; working out of the villages of Dabburiya and Hiobat –Lidd. A wind-blackened Flight sergeant at the wheel made his way inside. "I'm looking for an Irishmen, Sergeant Doyle. I'm told he's here", he said casting his eyes on Owen.

"That's me. What can I do for you Flight Sergeant?"
"I'm told you're the best instructor in Palestine on the use of machine and Bren guns. Will you have a look at the Bren gun moorings on the jeep to improve our accuracy?"
"Sure bring the jeeps round the back and we'll go for a practice run." He added," Jim look out for that leave for me," as he rose to meet the jeeps on the desert track. To the north and west the desert opened into a creamy-coloured void to the south a series of buildings and khaki tents met the eye. Owen examined the gun placements and adjusted the sights. He sat next to Israel Kazan, the Jewish gun operator. Nothing had disturbed Owen quite so much as the hatred between Arabs and Israelites. He knew nothing of the fact that a generation earlier his father had formed an unbreakable relationship with a Jewish emigrant. He thought he ought to be used to it, he ought to understand. After all was it so different from

Catholics and Protestants and nationalists and republicans? But strangely he didn't. Funny when the problem was someone else's it was difficult to fathom why they could not settle their differences. Was it about land or possessions? He liked the Jews, well organized creative, resourceful people. But he also liked the Palestinians, even in abject poverty they held on to their beliefs. Both were looking for the "promised Land."The Catholics of Northern Ireland in the early days looked to the Catholics of the south to help them reach the "promised land". The trouble was the Arabs and Jews wanted the same piece of land. In the end when the talking had stopped, the silence brought the storm. For a moment he remembered leaving Ireland, just as the Republican Army, led by Liam Lynch had tried to take the British Army at Mallow. The resulting Anglo-Irish treaty merely served to exacerbate the problem and civil war broke out. All Owen could really remember was the cycle of atrocities that broke out on both sides. Did we ever get it right? Even when Lynch was killed and the civil war over, things did not really change. Would he ever go back or had he drifted into perpetual exile? If he was homesick it was for the mountains and green pastures and sea pinks and a plate of colcannon. But something tugged at him; who was dead who was alive; a desire to see Connor, a desire to settle the differences with his mother; and was there still something between him and Marion. Was the way he felt real or an illusion? Army life was not conducive to having stable family relations. Besides how would he be received? An Irish catholic in the British Army did not exactly go down well. Could he fairly call Ireland his home again? Maybe meeting Marion would bring closure.

The Flight Sergeant drove the jeep to the far end of the practice range. Owen followed in a land rover. The wind had sharpened and stirred the sand along the sand dune crests. The Jewish soldier readied to fire at a small moving target on a rail track. The jeep moved off and commenced firing. Two thirds of his shots missed the targets, dragging clouds of desert dust around them as they travelled the hundred yards to the end of the practice range." Okay", said Owen, "One you are not balanced when you shoot. Sit back and position your legs so. Keep your body in line with the gun's barrel. Okay try again."On the re-run seventy five percent hit the target. The jeep swung away with a celebratory wave to Owen and went for a third run. Owen made his way to the Administration Block; the searing heat of the day pierced the uniform on his back. He wondered what the chances of leave would be. Jim McCabe met him at the door." No promises but I can swing two maybe three nights leave for you. There's an Ensign A27, four prop, leaving Jaffa in two hours bound for Valetta, Malta. So get your stuff and be back here in forty minutes."

"Right you are sir."Owen left hardly able to believe his luck. He packed quickly. He stuffed a civvies suit in his bag just in case the uniform didn't go down too well. By the time he had stuffed his possessions in to his canvas bag, taken a substantial loan from the Paymaster, he arrived back at the Admin Block to find a land rover and driver waiting. "Jim, thanks"

"You can thank me by being back here on Friday night. Oh I've booked you into the Hotel Phoenicia, a grand old place. The Barracks are all full. Things are hotting up and with the fleet being brought up to Malta something big is about to happen. Don't let me down!"

"The fleet is going to Malta?" said Owen concerned.

"No time Owen, get yourself on that plane," replied Jim half -knowing that the world was about to be turned on its head. The Warrant Officer thrust the papers and tickets into his hands and the driver and Owen moved off in the direction of Jaffa Airport.

Marion finished wrapping the bandage around the upper arm of a young infantry soldier, one of the Worcestershire Regiment's latest casualties. He winced with pain. "Right Nurse Gregson you can take over now."Marion stood a few minutes watching the nurse proceed. "Good well done". She wandered back to the Admin office. She had recently been promoted to Sister from her Staff nurse position at the Queen Alexandra Imperial Military Nursing Service. Her posting to the Mtarfa Military Hospital in Malta, originally opened in 1917, had been fast tracked owing to the shortage of personnel with expertise in dealing with malaria. Marion had specialised in tropical illnesses and was the ideal candidate. From that moment on the hill with Owen she had made up her mind to take control of her life. She had absconded from the Work house on that day, leaving for London, having seen an advert for trainee nurses at Chelsea Infirmary. Her dead father's reputation got her the job. She had worked hard for three years gaining her nursing qualification and now attaining the dizzy heights of Sister. From her apron pockets she pulled out the cable gram and reopened it on the desk. It merely said,

"Arriving today I'll find you." She wondered how he knew where she was, and how would she explain the passage of time. What had happened over the last fourteen years? Why in all that time had he only sent the odd postcard saying hallo? She knew it was him from the little blue flower which appeared in place of a signature. Why had she sent only one letter? Strange he always left an inkling of where he might be? Did he just want space and not isolation? Or had he found someone else? Why not? She had. Why should he be any different? Maybe tonight she would find out. She wondered what to say about his mother or if he still wanted to know. Owen's mother and Marion had managed to have several deep conversations and Marion was now beginning to piece together the trail of events that took Owen's father and Liam to America. Still realism took over what would she wear and where would they go? For God sake how will he find me?

The EnsignA-27, touched down with the deftness of a painter's brush, at Valetta airport a few hours later. It parked up by three Gladiator Fighter aircraft named Faith, Hope and Charity, the main air defense of Malta. The journey was swift and smooth. The only companions on board were two warrant Officers and a cabin full of over-full mail bags. The irony was not lost on him, that in all that time away he had written so little, and now he would arrive with a million letters. A jeep was waiting. Jim, I owe you. He thought. The driver a Geordie whose lyrical tones indulged in idle chatter throughout the six mile journey telling him where the best bars were, off handedly mentioned growing unrest around Germany's borders. But Owen was only half listening, his mind on other things. Before he knew it he had settled into his room and lay on the bed wondering what to do next. It was just three o'clock in the afternoon and he was nervous. His mind buzzed with excitement about seeing Marion, but a slight niggle surfaced from time to time over Jim's comment that the fleet was being called to Malta. The ceiling fan whirred above his head pushing large blasts of air heated by the mid -day sun around the room. He knew he couldn't lie still. He switched on the small radio left on the bedside table. Half listening he caught the tail end of a discussion over the movements of German troops and concerns about what Hitler was up to. Suddenly the newscaster went berserk declaring that information had just been received that German troops were massing on the borders of Sudetenland and this could only mean that massive repercussions would take place. Owen sat up trying to take in what had just been said. Jim must have known he thought. We're all in trouble now he thought. He knew he had little time to contact Marion. He quickly shaved and went down the stairs to the small reception area, with a bar overlooking the entrance, with views over the city and the fortifications of the Grand Harbour. Outside he noticed the jeep was still parked up and driver quietly sleeping in the back. He stirred as Jim approached. He nodded and the driver offered Owen a cigarette. Owen shook his head.

"I'm trying to find a place Mtarfa H. Might be a hospital?"

"Yes know it well. You wanna go?"

"Is it far?"

"No where's far in Malta. Ten minutes"

126

"Why not "Owen smiled, not believing his luck.

" Hop in .Names Frank."Owen shook his hand "Nice to meet you Frank. Owen" he said.

"Good to meet you too Owen. Irish are yer" The jeep turned around and headed off.

"Yes." said Owen a little guarded.

"Are yer here for training or stationed here?"

"Meeting an old friend. Two days leave. Got to find her first"

"Is she a nurse?"

"I don't know, probably her father was a doctor. Her names Marion"

"Marion! I picked up a nursing sister about three weeks ago from the airport dropped her at Mtarfa .You'll be able to contact her at the nurses reception at the back of the hospital. Lovely looking girl you lucky man"

Minutes later they arrived. Owen climbed out of the jeep."Thanks Frank."

"My pleasure, call me if you need me," handing him a well worn card with a number scribbled on it.

Owen watched the jeep disappear then leant against the wall suddenly aware of what he was doing. He had only shaved. Not taken a shower or changed his clothes. He wanted to look good for her. What was he doing? He must look terrible. He cursed himself. He was torn between the excitement of finding her and wanting the moment to be perfect. Should he go back or stay? In the end the decision was made for him. A group of five noisy, laughing auxiliary nurses, just coming off the night shift, came bursting through the open side door. He was almost trampled in the exodus as he skipped out of the way. Sorry they all shouted. Following behind was

Marion. Owen stood with his back to her."Owen is it you?"

Owen, felt a pang of emotion shoot through his body, a mixture of elation and sadness, a bitter sweet second till he turned around to see her. Marion was already wiping away happy tears. "Marion! Marion!" and before he knew it they embraced and kissed and for that moment he felt as if he had come home. For moments and moments he held her as tightly as he could, trying to wash away the time, wondering why he'd ever let her go. They breathed each other in and for moments both found it hard to speak until a voice broke the silence. "Oy! Cut it out you two." a porter said jokingly as he passed. They both relaxed ,laughing with excitement and nervousness. They held each other again and Owen said, "It's really good to see you."

"And you Owen." Marion kissed him on the cheek.

"You look wonderful."

"I feel wonderful." Her eyes sparkled.

Suddenly excited she grasped his arms . "Have you eaten yet?"

Owen stared into her green eyes mesmerised, he slowly shook his head, not taking his eyes off her." Let's get a coffee or a tea. I know this great little cafe. It's not far." She grasped his hands and he naturally followed. They fell down the narrow, winding, white-washed side streets, laughing and holding, blanking out for a moment the decade and a half of time that had stood between them. As they passed the Castille Hotel, a sixteenth century delight with its high facade and ornamental figures running along its front, the Ta Riccardu restaurant came into view, neatly tucked into the corner but exuding all the personality of its neighbour. Outside a bill board displayed a menu of dry-aged beef, fish, sundried tomatoes and capers. Owen pondered the eye-catching menu, wondering if a soldier brought up on army rations and full of nervous excitement still had the stomach to eat such a feast. Faris, the owner's son, and Chad the Maltese owner greeted Marion as if they had known her all her life."Madame Marion welcome again. Tell us who your fine friend is. Come sit down."Chad greeted her taking both her hand and kissed her on both cheeks. Faris tried to do the same but Chad waved him away. Faris wiped the wooden chairs inviting them with his eyes to sit down. Marion introduced Owen as if only a moment of time had passed since she last saw him on the hills above Cambletown. In truth not a day had passed without her thinking of Owen. Chad's three daughters tumbled into the restaurant, from the kitchen. The restaurant was now quickly filling up. They placed crisp-breads and humous on the table, laughing and shouting in Greek at each other, eying and talking about Owen. But Owen only had eyes for Marion. Marion ordered for both of them. Quietness returned to the restaurant as they strolled back to the kitchen. Owen fumbled with the crisp-bread and followed Marion's lead in dipping a corner into the humous bowl. He began awkwardly, knowing what he wanted to know but unsure if it would cause any pain. "Can you tell me what happened after I left." Marion took a deep and silent breath. " Well Joe..." "Don't tell me about Joe yet. What about yourself?"Marion looked away for a moment.

" Well you're the reason why I'm here. Your leaving made me realise that my life was a mess. I left the Workhouse the following morning and with my remaining money travelled to Chelsea where I was accepted on a nursing training course. Luckily it included accommodation in some pretty dire single billets off Westminster Road. I progressed and got posted to Mtarfa, Malta. Four weeks ago."

"You progressed. What, are you a Sister now ?"

"Matron. Newly promoted"

"Matron that's astonishing," said Owen in admiration.

" It wasn't your fault Owen, you didn't kill Matt. "Marion delivered the outburst looking directly into Owen's eyes

"What do you mean?"

"Joe was supposed to get the doctor. But he got drunk and tried to get O'Leary to drive him. O'Leary had problems of his own storing the guns, and wouldn't go. Joe had a set to with O'Leary and came off worst. He collapsed outside O'Leary's farm gate where Connor found him. They were all surprised to see Connor carrying Joe as they thought Joe was on his way for the doctor."

"How do you know all this?" Owen asked.

"Connor told me just before I left for Chelsea. He wanted to know if I knew where you were. He was scared and I felt uneasy about telling him too much. He wished me luck and said he was thinking of leaving also. From that day till now I have not seen Connor."

"What about Liam?"

"Liam was captured and arrested by the Tans, some time ago. Before the night you ran the moor."

"Has anyone seen him?"

"Not since you left. Emigration is high. More family's everyday see their loved ones immigrate to America he's only one among many faces missed. You know he continued working for Clan Na Gael don't you."

"I had an inkling. I knew he fell out with my Da just before he died, over what to do with the money. He hated being controlled. I heard that he wasn't happy with Irish Catholics fighting for the British Government. De Valera has certainly moved it on .Ireland is our new name for the twenty six counties; it's a Republic in all but name. I hear all reference to the British Crown has been removed from all state documents. If war comes in Europe, and it is coming, Ireland will be neutral. There's talk De Valera is about to buy ten torpedo boats from the British Government to protect the coastline. What a joke we'd be better off with the Royal Navy. He paused letting the current weighty problems of the world subside and returned to what he needed. He momentarily felt nervous of what the answer might be. "How are my mother and sister?"

"Both miss you very much. Your mother has had bouts of illness, and your sister is a wonder. She has taken full responsibility for the farm and has turned it around. They both long to see you and your mother tell me she has much of importance to share. She said she has much to show me concerning what your father wanted for you."

"She didn't say what?" Marion leaned forward and grasped his hand. Owen felt comforted that the farm was working, knowing most Catholics north or south of the border suffered chronic unemployment and what that meant for any family. Families needed each other he thought to stay alive. He quickly thrust the fifty pounds of money newly acquired from the Paymaster into Marion's hand. "Take this. Give it to my sister. It' not much."

Marion understood immediately. "It may be a little time before I'm home."

Chad arrived and removed some of the empty plates. "Come my friends be happy. The sun shines. Make the most of your time," but he already knew the world would never be the same again.

For a passing moment Owen became pensive wondering if he had made the most of his time. Where had the time gone? Why had he left it so long? What were his feelings for Marion and what did she feel about him? Was she waiting for him to make a move? The moments were passing faster than he could think. What did she expect of him? Events had moved on .He had seen new horizons, new futures and had begun to have different dreams. Ireland had turned him out at the moment of his greatest need and yet he wondered if he had got it all wrong? Was it just another mistake of humanity? Time alone would reveal how things would become. But whatever happened he knew like young children we all grow out of our clothes and when we go back nothing fits the same. Ireland was changing. Marion was changing. He was changing but not all together. His fleeting reverie was broken when Marion reached out and took his hand. As Owen reached forward to take both hands she moved her leg and it softly, almost imperceptibly touched his ankle. Owen's eyes glanced down, but he did not move his leg. Chad returned placing more crisp breads between them and moved away smiling to him. "What a feast," Owen blurted out and this helped to pass the moment and cover his indecision. He looked across to Marion. He was torn. Whichever way he turned he could find no sanctuary. He had kept the doors closed on all his feelings from the moment he had left Ireland and now seeing Marion's eyes he felt his heart was being prised open. Worse, he did not know where the conversation was going or if he could bear to travel the path. She met his gaze with a smile. Marion took the lead. "So you're a sergeant. You've done well. You've worked your way up .Not bad for a southern Irish, catholic boy. You must be good." Owen laughed to himself realising this was the first time an Irish voice had complimented him on doing well in the British army. He played it down however. He felt assured he'd done well but didn't want to jinx the future by believing it was true. Usually he was wary of taking compliments, but for some reason felt at ease, even pleased realising it was important to him. Owen held the plate of new crisp breads towards Marion. "So you're based here now?"

"Only for a little while. It's a staging post, while the team gathers together and then we'll be shipped out to wherever we are needed.

"Have you been to the Grand Harbour?" said Marion changing the course of the conversation. "No not yet," said Owen

"Drink up! We're doing a whistle stop tour."Marion's eyes lit up with excitement and mischief. The sun was high in the sky and extended a powerful heat across the street. Marion drank her wine in a few gulps and they headed off down the nearest back street. As they walked off hand in hand Owen noticed the amount of traffic converging on the streets leading to the Grand Harbour. He knew that the quarter of a million inhabitants of Malta totally depended on all their resources and food being brought in by sea. Especially petrol was hard to get. The smell of bread still lingered in the air from the first bake of the day as they sauntered down Old Bakery Street. The slate paved pathways lead down low-stepped alley ways and passed red painted British post boxes. The palm-lined streets gave way to Lascaris Wharf. As they rounded the corner of a small market, a black cat streaked out in front of them making them stop and take in the spectacular fortifications and vast panorama of the bay that opened up before them. Owen wondered if it would bring him luck. This majestic Grand Harbour expanded, separating the capital city of Valetta from the historic towns of Vittoriosa, Senglea and Cospiccia. Guarding its entrance two small forts, and in between two breakwaters with small lighthouses illuminating the way. In the bay, bobbing in the early evening light, two flying boats, a convoy ship with a newly delivered cargo of grain coal, cotton seed and Australian beef and two landing crafts bearing the insignia of the King's Own Malta Regiment. Owen mentally noted how insignificant these fortifications would be if war broke out. The island's strategic location made it centre stage in any theatre of war in the Mediterranean. They'd need more than Faith, Hope and Charity to survive what might be coming. I hope Marion's moved before then, not realising how much she was always in his thoughts.

The early evening darkness began to fall across the Grand Harbour and they began to make their way inadvertently back towards Owen's hotel. A small light illuminated their way down a narrow side street. It turned out to be a Greek tavern called the Falcon Bar. As they passed the strains of Bing Crosby singing "where the blue of the night, meets the gold of the day, someone..." spilled out of the door. As if unsure what to do next, Owen blurted out," Fancy a quick one?" Not really knowing if he did or not. Marion surprisingly answered, "Why not?" hugging Owen closer. As soon as they entered the small entrance hall, Owen out of the corner of his eye noticed three army soldiers looking the worse for drink, and began to regret his suggestion. Marion and Owen sat in a discreet corner but had been spotted by the loudest of the three soldiers who shouted across," Now don't hide you away! Don't I know you?" Owen knew that the soldier wasn't interested in him but in Marion, who wouldn't want to chat to a pretty girl, especially a stunningly pretty girl.

While Owen ordered drinks Marion began again to explain about Joe's death. "I know Joe probably got all he deserved, and I know he treated you badly but he died an agonising death. He was tortured before they shot him." Owen waited before he made a comment.
"How was he found?"
"He was found by Father Ryan and the Curate walking along the road to your farm. Joe had not been seen for two days before that, so they thought he may have been drunk and was lying hurt along the way. From the tyre tracks it was clear he had been brought by car to the spot and shot near the ditch. Long after the funeral, rumours were rife that a note had been found, pinned, on the body

with the words 'Here lies a traitor to Ireland. Death to all informers'. It was signed the IRA. "

"What Joe a traitor? I know he was a fool for a man but he loved Ireland dearly," said Owen never believing he would come to defend someone he had come to hate.

"It looked like an execution and had all the hallmarks of a Republican killing." Marion continued.

"Joe was a liability, he was apt when drinking to let slip what he knew. Not that I ever heard him give important information away."

"Father Ryan like you didn't believe it either; apparently he removed the note before your mother saw Joe's body."

Owen winced inside not wishing to associate his thoughts with those of some controlling priest."Why who does he think actually killed Joe?"

"He reckons it was the likely the work of some Auxiliary squad still active in the area."

Owen nodded, knowing that was probably right, these squads of returning Army Officers, known as Auxiliaries had become ruthless assassins of anyone who challenged their authority.

"How did my mother take it?"

"Like she was expecting it, like it was retribution for something she had done wrong." Owen was baffled by the words and could not understand what had happened to her. Before he could answer a distant cry intervened. "Hallo-oo. Are you too good to talk to us? "

Owen paused, realising any response would prompt further comment. But he had no alternative. "We're just having a quiet drink " Owen knew what was coming next.

136

"So what part of Ireland are you from?"

"A beautiful part with green fields , flowing rivers and good people"

The biggest soldier , the most inebriated, answered "So what's a man from southern Ireland doing in the British army". The soldier stood up as if to move forward. " I see your friend is from Northern Ireland." responded Owen

"But British by birth." the friend answered. Owen stood up .

"When I joined up no-one said who do you want to fight side by side with. Do you have any objections to fighting with an British man? It's a soldiers loyalty, the men he fights and dies with that transcends all nationalities. Who knows why I joined up ,Irish men north or south of the border have joined the British Army for centuries. Like them I had no work , no money and I was starving. You know what hunger is like. Surely there's room enough for all of us. Besides we may be fighting side by side sooner than you think. Now let me buy you a small drink, no offence but you've had a couple already."

The big soldier sat down, either overcome with the amount he had drunk, or the words Owen had expressed. In between, Owen had already signaled to the bar waiter to furnish them with a further drink. Quietly Owen and Marion made their exit and drifted in the direction of Owen's hotel. "Sorry about that." Owen remarked awkwardly

He realised what Marion meant to him and now was not sure what to do . What were Marion's feelings for him? Did they still have feelings for each other ? " You spoke well." Marion then decided to make his mind up by suggesting having a coffee in his hotel. Before he knew it he was standing at the lift to take them to his third floor room. As they entered his room , Owen pulled her close and kissed her. She returned his kiss. They moved towards the made up bed. Embracing they sat on the edge and gently lay together "I've missed you, really missed you. Oh Why did'nt I stay ? " Before Marion could answer a loud banging nearly demolished the bed room door.

"Sergeant Owen Doyle , Sergeant Doyle can we speak. Its the RM Police ." The knocking continued.

Owen in a state of confusion rolled to the other side of the bed, " Coming." The knocking continued. Owen snatched open the door to see Two RMP officers in dark navy uniform, white waist belts and red rimmed hats standing to attention.

"What can I do for you gentlemen," Owen a little concerned opened up.

"Sergeant Doyle ?" Owen nodded. "We are here to escort you urgently to the airport, the plane is fueled and waiting to take you back to Jaffa, at the request of your commanding officer."

"What's going on gentlemen?"

"You've clearly not heard but we are now at war with Germany. Come sir we need to go."

Shaken , Owen turned to find Marion stood behind him. " Sorry my darling I've got to go." Owen pulled her close and they kissed a last time."Stay safe. I love you "

"I love you too " came the reply

"Do you know where I'm bound after Jaffa" he said to the red hats

"As far as we know Sergeant your bound for South East Asia, Singapore to be exact"
He looked with dismay at Marion. "I'll write I promise," half knowing it may be a promise he can't keep.

'

Chapter 6

Five Points Ghetto: New York 1907

A star rising in the east'

The air was thick with smoke billowing from the nearby blacksmith's forge, nestled between a small distillery and a stable block, down the road from the tenement accommodation. Edmund awakened by the sharp bursts of sunlight, flashing through the clouds of drifting smoke and the tap of the blacksmith's hammer filling the room, stirred from his bed. His head ached through lack of sleep and he rubbed the pain from his eyes. Blinded for a moment he pulled the shutter across the window, deflecting the light and smoke entering the room. In the distance he could see, on high, like a Roman temple, in mid-town Manhattan, the Knickerbocker Trust Company headquarters. Four great Corinthian columns stood at its front; and of late Gunter and Edmund posing as interested customers had waited inside at chairs with desks, surrounded by Norwegian marble, bronze doors and mahogany tables. The building exuded a sense of seemingly lasting grandeur.

Christmas had passed and the cold of winter had abated. Liam had recovered well and recounted his knowledge of Sean Kenny. "Kenny is a Tipperary man, hard as cold steel. He's a liaison between Sinn Fein and Clan Na Gael. He carries large quantities of money between America and Ireland. He's fanatical and has killed for the cause. Last I heard he was in San Francisco. He's nationalist to the core. Be careful Edmund he's a dangerous man."

"Life is dangerous", Edmund thought, but sensibly took the information on board. He knew he and Gunter had too much pressing work. They all knew they had to take risks as Clan Na Gael would not take failure for an answer. They both had spent hours studying the financial and local news for the weeks and months, since Christmas. Like wheat gleaners they had sifted through every grain of information they could lay their hands on. Gunter had made a good network of financial "informers", now connected by a growing telephone system. They had spent what seemed like a life time in the bucket shop, watching the spread of rising and falling shares. They knew the value of information and its impact on the markets. They knew the bearing of the Schofield mining disaster on the price of coal. Only last year the April earthquake had devastated large parts of San Francisco, contributing seriously to market instability, prompting large sums of money to flow from New York to San Francisco to aid reconstruction. No doubt Kenny had his fingers in that pie. It was further exacerbated when the Bank of England raised interest rates in response to United Kingdom insurance companies paying out so much to American policy holders. Stock prices tumbled eighteen percentage points. Even small movements had grave repercussions.

Edmund had kept saying "what we are looking for is a rising star, a commodity in short supply; or perhaps some group who are trying to corner the market." They knew that a small group of wealthy bankers or entrepreneurs could through aggressive purchasing of stocks create a squeeze on the market, driving up share prices. The strategy of finding a rising star was dangerous. It depended on entering the market low and taking profits before any down turn in the market. It took nerve and wit to leave the market at the right time. Easy money and greed often overtook the naïve trader waiting too long to take profits and finding they were only left with a bag of dust. Gunter and Edmund both knew that one slip, one wrong judgment, and all their money, and all Clan Na Gael's money would be lost. Failure focused Edmund's mind on what needed to be done, but a small part of him plotted an escape route. But he hadn't found one yet.

It was Gunter that spotted the 'rising star'. In early May, Gunter had noticed fluctuations in the price of copper, and for some reason was now edging upwards. They were both aware that new technologies, phone lines, electric machines, petrol cars all needed increasing amounts of copper. They had also watched the big players, the Rothchilds, the Rockefellers affect market stability by trying to control the world copper market. When they teamed up together six years earlier to form Amalgamated Copper they had made Butte in Arizona the 'richest hill on earth'. By then the Rothchilds had control of over forty percent of copper production. Rumours abounded that the Rockefellers big in oil in Alaska, had found huge deposits of copper in Kennecott.

Edmund and Gunter knew they had found a 'rising star'. But would it last or rise far enough? What sealed their excitement was the column in the Wangamui Chronicle, that stated that all copper mines in and around Sydney, Australia would be idle owing to a strike of employees asking for higher wages. Short supply would likely drive the share price up even higher. Would it get out of control? What frightened Edmund was the feeling that this was a set up, and who was trying to do what in the market. Edmund was soon to find out.

It was Liam that drew Edmund to the other major event that had slipped unnoticed under Edmund's nose. "Are you having a flutter then", Liam offhandedly threw in to the conversation one afternoon.

"A flutter? On what?"

"A flutter on the Derby! The Kentucky Derby!" Liam threw down a used newspaper with all the riders and horses displayed. Edmund winced inside. He could afford no distractions, let alone distractions that excited him. He put the paper to one side and then found himself in unguarded moments glancing over the runners. Another distraction even more important to him than he imagined was about to disturb his concentration. He wondered why he or Gunter had failed to notice the increased trade in the bucket shop. Clan Na Gael had really focused their minds. The Kentucky Derby, how could he forget the most 'exciting two minutes in sport'? He knew it was also called the 'Race for the Roses', for the blanket of roses draped across the winner, and it was taking place on Saturday. This Saturday! The timing between the race and the shares rising couldn't have been any closer. In some ways it was a godsend. A large crowd would not only bring large amounts of cash but also give them some anonymity. For Edmund had to consider, if all went to plan, how he would carry out of the bucket shop the anticipated large bundle of notes. He glanced again at the runners. Red Gauntlet, Ovelando, Zal, Wool Sandals were all good three-year old thoroughbreds. He knew this was the final event in the Kentucky Derby Festival, and the first leg of the Triple Crown. Being only ten furlongs, the race was over before it had begun. It was not a race for hanging around. Before he became engrossed in the details Gunter reminded him, "Edmund, interesting as it is, we've got better things to do."

"Ay you're right"

Mary entered through the back door, "Right about what?"

"The race" responded Edmund looking up. He pulled a face. "You look wet"

"Wet it's pouring out there. It's coming up from the south west, from dear old Kentucky. The race'll be a wash out if it continues."

For a moment, Edmund was in Ireland, astride a three year old filly cantering across the lower slopes of the Galtee Mountains, in the pouring rain. Mary broke his reverie. "Are you not going to open it?" The corner of his mouth dropped. Another distraction loomed. "Open what?" he answered as he tried to lift a hot coffee, brought by Gunter, to his lips. Mary wouldn't be drawn, but merely flashed her eyes across the room to the letter carefully placed days before on the accountancy desk. Edmund shook his head slowly, struggling to get the coffee in his mouth. In the early hours of one morning

Edmund had written a letter to the Principal of Dunwoody Seminary College, recounting the loss of the Introductory Letter. Weeks had passed with no response from the college. Then a few days ago, it finally arrived. A letter bearing the raised college crest, like some Papal greeting, was left at Gunter's store. Edmund turned the letter over and over, placing it down on the accounting desk, making coffee, returning to touch but not to open. He dreaded what the response would be .Either way, you have a place, your place is no longer available, he was uncertain how he would deal with the outcome. Mary seized the moment and offered to open it. Edmund started to say something but stopped, he took a second to collect his thoughts, then he nodded. Mary opened the letter, read for a few moments. "Well?" said Edmund, his voice lacking conviction.

"The Rector, Most Reverend John Levine is offering you an interview and a chance to explain yourself on Friday 5th May3-00pm. She held the letter out. Edmund took the letter and read for himself. He felt numb and tears welled in his eyes. Mary embraced him half- knowing what he was going through. Edmund suddenly blurted out, "But that's this Friday! I can't go."

"But you must." Mary responded without thinking.

Gunter looked baffled. "Are you worried about Saturday?"

"I don't want any complications" Gunter gritted his teeth, knowing that the priority was to make sure Saturday went well. The alternative was unthinkable. Suddenly there was a sharp knock on the back door and Sean Kenny strode in. He was alone or rather his protection waited outside. "Good morning gentlemen", touching his imaginary hat as the greeting fell. His long coat shimmered with raindrops, "Looks like it'll be wet on Saturday". Edmund nodded wanting to keep the conversation short. Kenny moved in amongst them like a tiger choosing his dinner. He picked up Edmund's half filled mug and swallowed the coffee. He ran his finger along the accounting desk looking for dust and raised his eyebrows when he found none. Liam entered the room and looked across to Edmund but got no response. "Welcome back to the land of the living Liam," Kenny responded, enjoying the moment. "Gentlemen, to business. The three thousand dollars, courtesy of Clan Na Gael will be with you on Friday night. Find somewhere for its safekeeping. Remember we'll be watching!" Edmund had learnt how to respond to Kenny not to get too drawn in. He knew better than to ask 'what time' and merely responded, "We'll see you when we'll see you then".

"You will indeed," Kenny retorted as he headed for the door, stopping only to take a sugared almond from a counter jar. "Very fine, I know someone else who likes sugared almonds", as the door closed. The apprehension in the room was palpable. Mary sat down slowly in one of the desk chairs. Edmund left the room. Liam poured a glass of beer. Gunter screwed the lid back on the sugared almonds jar. Upstairs they could hear furniture being moved about. Edmund returned with a smallish leather suitcase, discreet enough not to cause attention, big enough to hold twenty five thousand dollars in fifty dollar bills. Edmund looked around at the concerned faces. A bright smile lit up his face "Okay. Let's go through what we have to do in the next few days".

146

The next morning the New York Times contained photographs of the thousands of race goers making their way to Louisville, including the prominent Congressman, Nicholas Longworth and his wife. An air of anticipation thronged the streets even in the Five Points. It was a slow, quiet day in the store. The nervousness continued but they all threw themselves into work of one kind or another. While Mary and Megan made dresses Edmund and Liam paid one last visit before Saturday to the bucket shop. It was full to bursting with overexcited punters. Edmund and Liam stood in the door entrance going over in their minds the sequence of events of how to bring the money in and take the winnings out. Edmund spotted the silver-haired teller Bridie at the far counter dealing admirably with several agitated punters. She even had time to flash him a smile which he acknowledged. His scan around the room always lighted on the small group of men sitting in the corner by the door. He didn't recognize anyone but sitting at their feet on a makeshift wooden box was Stutter. Over time Edmund had got to know Stutter, realising he had got into bad company in order to survive, but recognizing that no one took him seriously. Deep down he was just a frightened kid. Stutter would have to do something monumental to be really noticed. Edmund took the small pack of sugared almonds out of his pocket and dropped them into his lap as he passed, exiting through the half- blocked door. "Thank you sir, good luck for tomorrow sir," he yelped. Edmund thought "We'll need it" and Liam noted what he had done and smiled.

Darkness had fallen during their time in the bucket shop, so Liam and Edmund made their way back to the rooms in the tenement block. Mary had food on the table by the time they arrived and announced her news. "Edmund ,Liam do you remember I wrote to my brother some weeks back, well he intends to arrive here in the next four days from Glens Falls, just up the Hudson, beyond Albany. He will then escort Megan and me back to his farm and store in Syracuse, near Lake Ontario." Edmund was dumb-struck; he put down his fork and looked around the table. In all his deliberations about the arrangements for securing the money for Clan Na Gael he'd forgotten what was really important to him. Edmund's mind was buzzing with the run of events happening and wondered how they would all fit together. He collected his thoughts. "Megan we must prepare a welcome for your brother John", with a momentary look at Mary, "Let's sort this tomorrow." Edmund responded."Tomorrow he thought to himself I must speak the Rector. The morrow after we pay off Clan Na Gael, and the morrow after that we celebrate John's arrival. What could go wrong! What indeed! As he thought he removed the cork from a bottle of wine and poured four glasses. Liam offered a toast, "May the road rise to meet us," and they talked of what they would do for John. Mary smiled and patted Edmund on the shoulder, he turned and put his arm around her and pulled her close. She knew there was much that was unsaid, much to do and much to pray for.

The driveway leading upwards, to the entrance of St Joseph's Seminary College, surpassed all of Edmund's expectations. Situated some ten miles west of the Five Points, Edmund had taken a train and walked the last two miles to where he now stood. Formally a military college and now a seminary, the original building had been razed to the ground by fire some eighty years ago. The entrance guarded by two huge towers, was supported by two extensive wings that expanded across the horizon and were capped by a vast Gothic revival church with spire and at the other far end a huge dormitory block. Grounds laid to grass with well-tended flower beds fell on either side of the gravel drive, which he crushed under foot as he made his way to the ornate entrance doors. A large cross dominated the entrance foyer. He felt a strange unease as he entered into a large open hallway. Looking round he caught the tail end of a small queue towards the back, being attended to by a man wearing a suit and dog collar. The lady in front of him inquired about whether being from a lowly background would hinder entrance to the college.

"No madam. We believe that God calls all people from all walks of life and that each person has a unique ministry to fulfill. How old is your son?" he added in a silvery voice.

"He's only seven"

"Not yet confirmed?"

"Soon to be."

"Then teach him the catechism and through your priest, come back when he's sixteen years old, if he believes God has work for him to do." Edmund found himself shuffling from one foot to the other; not wanting to hear; wanting to go; wanting to stay. He was disturbed by the answers in his head. Does God have work for me too? He was so engrossed in his own thoughts that he failed to notice the woman had left. "How can I help you?" a voice echoed in his head.

"Father, I have an appointment with the Rector the Most Reverend John Levine."

"Ah, Mister Doyle", he replied and looking up, continued, "thank you for coming. Please wait," pointing to two seats, "and the Reverend's personal assistant will attend you soon." Edmund moved in the direction of the seats, situated out of harm's way in a small alcove off the main stairs. "Thank you Father." Edmund murmured as he retreated into the quiet corner. Clean glasses and water were resting on a small table, along with pamphlets about the college. Edmund poured himself a glass of water, not realising how dry his mouth was. A few minutes passed, and then down the stairs, a small, suited and smiling man walked towards him. He held out his hand. "Mister Doyle," he spoke with a strong southern Irish accent, "Welcome to St Josephs. I am Gavan Duffy, personal assistant to the Rector. Edmund shook hands. "Mister Doyle, I will in a few moments take you up to the Rector's office. Now, the Rector in these unusual circumstances has arranged for a discussion with you and has invited two observers, one of the college's Major Superiors and a Diocesan Bishop from our church have kindly offered to attend. Have you any questions?

"Yes am I likely to get an answer today to my enrollment in the college".

"It's unlikely today .You will receive a letter in the next few weeks. That is of course pending the arrival of your Introductory Letter, which forms the contract between the college and your priest, as you know."Gavan looked

down at his notes. "Okay, follow me Mister Doyle." They made their way up to the top landing, and then along several carpeted corridors until arriving at a plain uninteresting door with the simple words 'Welcome' across the upper panel. As the door opened, a large room, with floor to ceiling windows; furnished with single chairs and a Victorian style sofa, placed around a carved stone fireplace came into view. To the side through two stained glass screens, two double doors signaled the entrance to a small chapel. The Rector a tall man, with thin silver hair, wearing a full priest dress, turned to welcome him. "Edmund, please make yourself at home," and offered a single high-backed chair carefully positioned so he could meet the gaze of the Major Superior and the Diocesan Bishop seated on the sofa. Edmund was introduced and began to ready himself for the spiritual interrogation to come. The early discussion concentrated on the loss of the Letter of Introduction and his early life in the Five Points. Their knowledge of the Five Points was profound and they recognized the immense poverty and hardship. Also it was a good place to find the odd one or two sinners. Edmund sensed they had not asked the difficult questions yet. They seemed to know something he didn't."Society is losing its sense of sin." The Rector continued, "We must all make the effort to recognize sin, in our daily actions, words and omissions. Have you continued to celebrate Mass, Edmund?"
"I have Father, twice a day>"
"Have you denied your faith?"The interrogation continued.

"I have not Father," Edmund responded robustly. The Rector persevered, "As a candidate for priesthood, we must examine the suitability and vocation of the aspirant. We must ask all the questions no matter how difficult, to help us make a decision. You understand."The Rector paused. "Have you belonged to a society for apostolic life?"

"No father, it was never presented to me."

"I'm finding your answers confusing Edmund. Disturbing news has reached us that you are working on behalf of Clan Na Gael. Is this true?"

Edmund looked up, so that's what it was. "I'm not working for Clan Na Gael. I find myself compromised and in order to save the people close to me, I am using my God –given skills to ensure their safe passage."

"Well said Edmund," the Rector retorted. But Edmund could see in their eyes that the answer had fallen on barren ground. "Thank you Edmund. We abide by the Code of Canon Law. We shall let you know in due course of our decision," as he glanced around the room at the other faces. Edmund rose from his chair, shook hands and left. He wasn't to know that the decision to enter college or not was in his hands or theirs. God's will was to be done by others.

When he got back, Mary, much as she was desperate to know, was sensitive enough to discern that Edmund would recount what had happened in his own time. She and Megan busied themselves with the arrangements for their brother's arrival. Both were excited. Mary and Megan had not seen John for two years. Mary also wondered if John would like Edmund, as it was very important to her. Gunter and Edmund worked all afternoon and into the small hours tracking the share price of copper. The only time he stopped was to attend mass, morning and night Something was going on so to quell their nerves they walked to the square on which most of the big banks were built. They stood in the entrance to the Knickerbocker Trust Company and watched the passing clientele. The price of copper was still rising and looked like reaching the level they needed sometime the following day. As they returned, they noticed the bucket shop was heaving. Two overexcited drunks were tipped out, by the overweight Chinese bouncer, like two dice on to the stone sidewalk. Gunter led the way back into the store to find Sean Kenny perched on the counter, legs dangling in the sacks of potatoes. "Gentlemen I bear gifts." On the other end of the store counter wrapped in cloth, lay a leather pouch. Gunter moved to pick it up but Kenny shook his head and placed a loaded revolver on the counter. "Firstly let's understand each other. Once you take the pouch be it on your heads if you fail. Now where will it go tonight?" Gunter responded "In the safe", pointing to a large cast iron fronted box under the counter. "Good, good, then I'll be back tomorrow for the winnings. Be ready. If anything happens, I will personally hunt each one of you down," and with that he picked up the revolver and pointed at each one of them in turn miming a shot between the eyes. Gunter was visibly angered when he pointed the gun at Anya. He moved to quell his anger and was thankful for Edmund's restraining hand on his shoulder. "Don't worry you'll have your money." Edmund interjected. Kenny jumped down from the counter, and made his way backwards towards the door, his gaze never left Edmund's eyes. As soon as he exited the door Gunter unwrapped the pouch, counted its contents and placed the pouch in the safe. "Five thousand dollars to buy shares; he'd never risked so much in all his life. His hands began to shake so much that he failed to lock the safe the first time. God be with you Edmund Doyle, he whispered to himself.

A fresh breeze was blowing the following morning. The rain of the previous day had subsided and Edmund taking a deep breath of cool air thought he could see blue sky on the horizon. He needed something to lift his spirits. He waited in the backroom for the others to assemble. They wandered in one by one. In his head he had prepared a speech, about that they could do this, but if it all went wrong he would be sorry he had failed them. He wanted them to know how important they were to him and that his life had been enriched by knowing them. As he looked round at their faces he realized all he could say was, "Well we are ready let's do it." The three, Gunter, Liam and Edmund carrying a smallish leather case wandered over to the bucket shop. Edmund stopped outside, gave his usual greeting to the Chinese bouncer. Glancing at Liam and Gunter, and breathing deeply through his nose, expelling the air slowly, he pushed the bucket shop door open. The rollercoaster had begun. The bucket shop, even three hours before the race, was bursting at the seams with punters. Edmund, followed by Gunter and Liam pushed their way through the mêlée of bodies. The fans above their heads pushed great hot flushes of cigarette smoke and air across their faces. The noise of the ticker-tape and outbursts of laughter drowned out the conversation between them. Edmund caught sight of Bridie, beset by punter demands, but she eventually wandered over to see them. "Come for the race?"

"No. Here to buy shares."

"Shares!" she almost laughed.

"I thought you'd be up for the race?"

"Maybe later."

"How many shares do you want to buy?"

"Three thousand copper shares"

She moved closer to Edmund and lowered her voice realizing the weight of the conversation. "You know that is four thousand, nine hundred and forty seven dollars?" More than some would earn in a year of work. "Yes. Can we do this in your office?"Bridie nodded and went to have a quiet word with one of the other bucket shop tellers who opened the internal office door. The three then entered and the money exchanged by a wide-eyed Bridie who had never seen such a wager. Edmund remained by the counter, as Liam and Gunter went to wait in the door entrance. In the corner the same unknown faces occupied were crouched on the bench seats, Stutter squatting on the floor beside them. Hollowlegs and the Stovepipe gang leader were nowhere to be seen. Edmund leaned on the counter knowing they had a few hours to wait, if all went well. The price of copper shares flickered on the ticker-tape, one dollar sixty five cents. When it reached their withdrawal target of four dollars they would hope to cash in. It was tricky because the deal was time limited and the earliest they could cash in was three thirty. Timing was everything. To pass the time Edmund scanned the horses in the races leading up to the Derby event. He knew he couldn't lose focus. Then he glimpsed the runners in the Kentucky Derby. Even if he wasn't going to bet he could at least choose the winner. He let his eyes drift across the names Zal, Ovelando, Red Gauntlet, Orlandwick, Wool Sandals, Boland, and Pink Star. Pink Star his eyes jolted back over the details. The name immediately conjured up memories of walking the Galtee Mountains. The sea pinks flourished on the upper slopes. Pink Star the words echoed in his head. He read further. Sired by Pink Coat, American Derby winner and grandson of Kentucky Derby winner, Leonatus, it appeared he had picked the winner. Until that is he noticed race tipsters had described Pink Star as a lumbering, ugly mount and not in the same class as Zal, the fancied favourite. He glanced around the room again, the ticker-tape fluttered and he noted the price of copper shares had edged up to two dollars. He tried to contain his excitement. Every now and then a wave of uncertainty washed over his mind. He knew if the banks caught a whiff of intrigue, they would close down on their lending, and this retraction of market liquidity would unnerve depositors, who demanding their money back would crash the market. He also knew that this could be exacerbated by unregulated side bets in a bucket shop, exactly what they were doing.

He looked across to Gunter and gave a thumbs up. Gunter realized the share price was rising and his mind flitted between excitement and panic and from time to time, he waited outside to cool off. Edmund noticed from the ticker-tape that someone was buying large amount of shares in the United Copper Company. He understood that to do this the buyers would need the backing of at least one of the large banks. The ticker-tape rattled again, two dollars twenty cents, a profit of one thousand six hundred and fifty two dollars after only an hour. By now he would have cashed in. He conveyed the message to Gunter who turned and went out of the door. Bridie looked across to Edmund a few times but he sensed that she knew something was up. The ticker-tape rattled again, copper shares had risen to two dollars forty cents, more profit than they had earned in the previous three months. Edmunds eyes flitted around the room again knowing others may notice the rise. He tried to appear unconcerned. The rollercoaster was about to get faster. He made his way through the crowd towards Liam and Gunter, "Keep smiling!" he said through gritted teeth. "Someone is buying big into United Copper."

"That must be Augustus Heinze, he has always wanted the controlling shares."

"Have a significant number of share been borrowed, do you think?"

"Maybe"

"Someone must be selling short, huge amounts of shares are being bought."

"You're right."

"The price is rising fast."

"Perhaps too fast," as Gunter said it, the share price had now reached three dollars.

Edmund returned to the counter. At the counter he often picked up leads from other people's conversations. The world turned around on these nuggets of information. He had already noted that Arcite and Boxara had been scratched from the field saying the 'going' was too heavy, leaving only six to compete. He looked again at the runners, and in more detail at Zal. He kept returning to Pink Star, hoping the news would get better the more he read. He had a good trainer W.H.Fizer, well regarded and no fool; but a lumbering, ugly mount was the sticking point. The ticker-tape rattled like a machine gun, and the share price rose to three dollars sixty cents. A fortune in profit .Edmund surmised at this rate it would rise above perhaps the five dollar mark before they could cash in. He wiped the small beads of sweat from his upper lip. He noticed Stutter re-enter the shop. He was ignored by the other gang members so he made his way to where Edmund stood. He seemed very agitated as if he had news to tell. Edmund placed a sugared almond in his hand. "Thanks Mister Doyle. You should see all the people outside!"

"Punters, for the big race?"

"No not around here!"

The ticker-tape signaled three dollars sixty cent. Edmund looked again."Sorry lad, not punters?"

Bridie's voice intervened across the tannoy, "Bets for the Derby will close at five to three."

"No, not p-p-punters."

"But not outside here."

"At the k-k- kerb market."

"Kerb market where?" said Edmund listening with all his concentration. The ticker-tape purred three dollars sixty seven cents. Edmund threw a look to Gunter who was clearly excited. 'Calm down Gunter' he said to himself. "Kerb market where?" He repeated to Stutter.

"Kerb market , n-n-nickerbocker t-t-rust." Edmund suddenly grabbed Stutter's shoulders, "Stutter you are

158

telling me that a big crowd is gathering outside the Knickerbocker Trust building." The ticker-tape clattered again three dollars seventy two cents. They had made eighteen thousand six hundred dollars. His heart started pounding, he knew he had only minutes, maybe his last minutes to keep him and those close alive. Gunter gave him the thumbs up. In a flash he knew what was happening. "Bridie if I resell the shares what will I get?" Bridie gave him a quizzical look, "You can only release the wager at the agreed time three thirty or lose the set up fee."

"What will I get if I do it now?"

"Why do you want to do that? You're on a winner."

"Bridie tell me what I would get!"

"Hold on, you lose six hundred dollars."She raised her head, "Why are you doing this? What going on?"

"I think the market........."His words trailed away

"I'll tell you what I want you to do." The ticker-tape rattled again three dollars seventy five cents. Edmund looked down at Stutter. "Stutter I need you to do something for me. Go and see what the crowds are doing now. I need you back as soon as possible." With that he gave Stutter the remains of the sugared almonds. Edmund didn't see the other gang members rough Stutter up as he passed through the door, heading in the direction of the kerb market. Bridie meantime had almost finished the paperwork that Edmund had asked for. Edmund waited now for Stutter to return. The seconds ticked by. Edmund knew it was a forlorn hope, he had to decide what he was going to do. The ticker-tape jangled again three dollars seventy eight cents. Beads of sweat fell down his temple. He wiped his face with the back of his hand. The tannoy buzzed again, "Gentlemen please place your bets for the Kentucky Derby, the counter will close in three minutes. Edmund leaned over to Bridie and whispered in her ear."Are you sure you want to do that?" She responded. Edmund gave one last glance back at Gunter and Liam who were in good spirits, stood by the door. Gunter however had noticed the tension in Edmund's face. "Is everything alright Liam ?" Liam glanced at Edmund and said, "Whatever's happening Edmund will make the best decision. We have to trust him. I do." Bridie's voice carried the final message for all punters, the counter was now closed. Three twenty eight ,the race was now on. Edmund gripped the counter, "Any chance of a coffee Bridie?" His mouth had suddenly gone dry. The ticker-tape rattle sounded the rise of copper to three dollars seventy nine cents. Stutter still had not returned, but he would never know how much help he had been. "And they're off. The Derby rallied to a good start." The voice commentary carried over the airwaves. "And the early leader is Wool Sandals. Jake Boland on Zal is a close second. The going is heavy the track is almost fetlock deep in mud." Edmund thought all that rain. The punters responded excitedly. The favourite Zal was leading the way. "And Zal is setting a stiff pace, with Wool Sandals and Ovelando alternating in second place. Red Gauntlet and Orlandwick see-sawed along and trailing six lengths behind Pink Star." the commentary explained. Some punters began to laugh thinking Pink Star was now out of it. The ticker-tape jangled again three dollars eighty four cents a share. Edmund held his breath. Would it rise or fall? Had he made the right decision? Only Bridie knew what he had done. "And here we are coming up to the mile post and Zal still leads the way. Ovelando is second. And making good progress on the stand side is Pink Star in fourth place." Murmurs ran around the shop. Stutter still had not returned. Suddenly the ticker-tape machine went berserk. Tape poured out at a furious rate. Copper shares were falling the bubble had burst. They never made four dollars a share. Something big had happened. No sooner had one burst of tape been reviewed another spewed out. For a moment the race was forgotten. Copper shares had fallen to three dollars fifty cents. Shouts of 'Come on Zal!' filled the shop. Thousands of people across America were acclaiming Zal the winner as the riders entered the final stretch. 'Come on Zal!' The ticker-tape purred like a cat. Copper shares had dropped to three dollars. Edmund knew the market was crashing. Gunter picked up the thread and screamed "Get the money out. The noise in the shop rose louder "Zal! Zal! Come on Zal." None had realized Andy Minder ,the jockey had uncoupled Pink Star, a big bay colt ideally suited to heavy going, had closed up four lengths between him and Zal, successively mowing down Wool Sandals and Ovelando with the greatest of ease. The ticker-tape whirred like a fan. Copper shares had crashed to one dollar fifty cents a share. Edmund tried to hear the commentary but sound of 'Come on Zal' drowned him out. He caught small pockets of commentary, 'Here comes Pink Star'............Zal has tried to match the speed........Ovelando is attempting to pass on the stand side." The ticker-tape screech to a halt declaring the market had crashed. Edmund and Gunter realized the shares were worth nothing. A quietness had fallen over the bar. Everyone had lost or so it seemed. Edmund spoke to Bridie who ushered him into the back room. Gunter and Liam moved through the crowd towards Edmund. But he was sharp with them. "Go back to the door that was the plan."

"But everything is lost", said Gunter.

"Not now Gunter, stick to the plan."Liam nodded and took Gunter by the arm, who gave no resistance. Over the radio the final commentary" And the winner of the thirtieth Kentucky Derby, by two lengths from Zal the course favourite, is Pink Star. With its long odds someone's a lucky boy tonight."Gunter and Liam did not hear the announcement as their minds were on other things. Edmund emerged from the back room seventeen minutes later, leather suitcase in hand. His hand trembled as he lifted the counter to pass through and move into the disappearing crowd. On reaching Gunter and Liam, the door was suddenly flung open and Stutter stood stock still with his hands and body covered in blood. The gang members bolted almost immediately through the open door as Stutter collapsed into Liam's arms. He had been shot in the shoulder. And then in a clear voice without a hint of a stutter, he said, "I've killed Sean Kenny. I've killed Sean Kenny."Sean Kenny was lying on the steps of the Knickerbocker Trust Company dying of a stab wound to the neck. "Don't talk," said Liam recognizing that stutter was fatally wounded.

"Now everyone will want to talk to me,"he said faintly and with that his head slumped to one side his eyes wide open. Liam shook his head and laid Stutter gently to the ground, closing his eyes as a final gesture. Two police officers took over from Liam inquiring who had he spoken to before he stabbed Sean Kenny. Liam confirmed that Sean Kenny was dead. By the time he had finished the conversation, Edmund and Gunter had already set off for the store. Gunter and Edmund were silent all the way to the store, both were stunned by the deaths of Stutter and Sean Kenny. It turned out that Stutter, challenged by the other members of the gang to do something useful, on recognizing Kenny, offered him a sugared almond and as he bent down to take it he was stabbed in the throat. The deaths changed everything. Who would now take over from Sean Kenny? When Liam returned fuller details began to emerge. It turned out that the Stovepipe gang leader, Red was also badly wounded shot by Kenny's armed guard. Rumours were rife that Edmund had made a fortune on the sale of copper shares. Edmund said nothing. The store was full when Gunter and Edmund returned. Both had set to helping Mary, Megan and Anya, recently up from the cellar kitchen having prepared for John's arrival, in dealing with customers. But Anya, Mary and Megan, could tell from their faces that things had not gone well. While no-one, that being Edmund, actually said, it was assumed that all the money was gone and what remained was how to explain the situation to Clan Na Gael. How would they repay the three thousand dollars? Edmund had wondered what the Reverend John Levine would make of the afternoons activities, for he would surely know. Would he pick up the rumours about his wager surely not? Edmund pondered how giving the sugared almonds to Stutter had caused Sean Kenny's death. God works in mysterious ways. What does he have in store for us? The answer was to come quicker than he thought.

No sooner had Anya locked the front store door, seeing the last customer out. When the back door opened slowly, almost without sound, and five men from Clan Na Gael entered the room. The leader appeared to be a small stocky man, with a burn mark across his forearm, stepped forward and spoke directly to Edmund. "You know what's happened! We now have a problem or maybe two problems? Firstly the money, we know the market crashed; and caused a run on the banks. The Knickerbocker will probably close. It's brokers Gross and Kleeberg are in real trouble. It's a fucking mess! So what is your position, Doyle? How much money is left? Edmund sat down at the accounting desk, the small leather suitcase resting in the middle. Gunter and the others looked on, anticipating the answer, waiting for the response. Liam surreptitiously, was feeling down the side of the counter for the piece of hardened wood placed there for dealing with awkward customers. From his chair ,Edmund spoke, "I think we agreed fifteen thousand dollars was the debt I owe Clan Na Gael." The stocky guy nodded. Edmund carefully opened the small suitcase and counted out on the table in crisp one hundred dollar notes, fifteen thousand dollars. Gunter and the others looked on in jaw-dropping wonder. He coughed hard and struggled to believe what he had seen. Liam relaxed his hand on the wooden weapon. The stocky man, Blake Dillon was equally startled. "How did this happen?" Edmund's reply was curt and to the point, "None of your business. My job was to get the money. Here it is? 'God forgive me' he said to himself.

"Well that's problem one solved! Problem number two. Who will take the money to Ireland now Sean Kenny is dead? He is due to leave on May 12th, six days away. Edmund paused for a moment, "I will!" He kept his eyes on the suitcase. Mary visibly shuddered and Gunter and Liam fell back against the counter. Is he joining Clan Na Gael? They both thought. "You will!" Dillon blurted out in astonishment.

"Yes. But I will speak with you in private for I have several conditions."

"Doyle you do surprise me!" He escorted Edmund to the other side of the room where they spoke in whispers. Liam for the first time in his whole life began to wonder about their friendship. He knew they needed the help of Clan Na Gael but this was more than they needed. Was this the Edmund he knew? After their conversation they returned to the others. The tension in the room had grown. Dillon had wandered over to a vase of roses and picked one out snapping off the bud. Returning, placed the rose in Edmund's jacket lapel, "We will abide by the conditions you state and be back in a few days. You deserve a garland of roses for your efforts but this will have to do. Nice doing business with you Edmund Doyle."

As soon as they were gone, silence returned to the room. Edmund knew he needed to clear the air. "I need to tell you what will happen. You are the most important people in my life. I could not have finer friends, compatriots and people I love. I have made arrangements for you safe passage to anywhere you wish to go. I will go back to Ireland. I need to explain to the priest and my father. I can only do this personally. The money is a gift from God who answered our prayers in time of need. Liam you need to decide if you wish to join me in going back. Gunter your store will have continued protection from the Stovepipe gang but they are probably a spent force now. Megan will be able to go with her brother tomorrow."

Gunter jumped in," I can't believe it! How much money did we make?"

"Fifty three thousand dollars." All were staggered. Mary however was very quiet and left the room unnoticed. Anya repeated over and over, "Fifty three thousand dollars," finding it hard to take in. "How did it happen?" A gift from God!" was all that Edmund would say. Even in the coming days he refused to explain. Gunter had already opened a bottle of wine. "Do you have to go to Ireland?"

"Yes I have explaining to do. Gunter will you sort out the money? I need to talk with Mary." Edmund found Mary in the kitchen. "I suppose this is all a bit strange, me offering to go to Ireland." Mary gave no answer. "Mary I need to say something. Something I've been meaning to say for months. Something I couldn't say while this danger hung over us. But Mary Carson." She looked up. "I do know I love you very much and can only go to Ireland if you come with me."Edmund moved towards her and gently took her hands and kissed both in turn. They embraced. "Mary Carson. Will you be my wife?"

"Yes," she whispered, "With all my heart."But she had more pressing news to tell him.

John arrived the following day, and he decided to stay longer so that he could say good bye to Mary. The next five days passed quickly, there seemed no time to do all they needed to do. Clan Na Gael honoured the arrangements agreed with Edmund. In no time they found themselves waiting at the docks ready to board a sister ship of the Lucania, this time with second class tickets. Clan Na Gael had provided ample protection. Liam had decided to stay in America at least until the fall. Mary said her goodbyes to her brother and Megan, tears fell between them. They both would set off in the coming days to Syracuse, near Lake Ontario. Mary and Edmund stood on the second class passenger deck waving to Gunter and Anya who knew this was the last time they would see their friends, for as one great adventure was over a second was beginning. A few days after the boat had sailed, a letter carrying a raised college crest, dropped through the letter box at Gunter's store.

Chapter 7

Easter 1942 Malaya
'Hunger, Hunger. Thou savage goad'.

The train carriage rocked violently as it passed over the points at the Cameron Highland's rail junction. Owen leant back against the bolted, sliding, carriage doors, his body soaked in sweat. A soldier held by his hands, dangled out of a make-shift hole in the side of the carriage, kicked out earlier, passing excrement along the track below. He moaned through pain and embarrassment not knowing he had the early signs of dysentery. Owen felt the bodies press in on him at every lurch of the carriage; all one hundred men forced into a cattle truck. It was clear not everyone would survive the journey. Most were standing almost touching each other. A few those too weak to stand or wounded, or recently beaten, sat in resigned groups with their knees hunched, trying not to occupy more space than they needed. Owen was grateful to lean against a small protruding lintel screwed to the carriage door, allowing him to take the weight off his feet. The tension in the carriage was palpable. The midday day sun made the metal stanchions blisteringly hot and having to breathe in the stench of unwashed bodies and excrement unbearable. Owen wiped the stinging sweat from round his eyes touching his bruised right cheek courtesy of a Japanese rifle butt. He was lucky it was only a glancing blow. He looked at

Jim McCabe, "Jim we need to get you sat down, your breathing is laboured, looks like you've broken a few ribs,"

"I'll be fine. There's worse here than me."

"At least, lean against this door." Owen deftly slipped across and holding him around the waist, lowered him onto the protruding lintel. Immediately the colour began to return to Jim McCabe's face. "Thanks." The train lurched again.

"Where are we now Owen?"

"We must be through the Cameron Highland's Junction; it should get cooler for a while."

"We passed through Kuantan an hour back. We seem to be travelling up the east coast of Malaya and have begun to cut across country heading for Thailand." Jim McCabe was a highly able officer destined for big things. He knew the territory like the back of his hand.

"Supply lines must be getting thin; the Japs are overstretched themselves and need to get resources to the front line. If the information is right and they have taken Burma, they'll need to get supply lines open as soon as possible." A blast of cooler air entered the carriage brought some relief but raised fears that another night in freezing temperatures would mean more deaths by morning.

"You're right they must control all the ground from Indo China to Singapore. Over that distance supply lines are bound to get overstretched. But why take us?"Jim looked down with resignation.

"Labour. They need labourers." Owen just took it in and through a small slit in the carriage door he could see sporadic fires, derelict buildings and almost every rail station was covered in fallen debris. At each station stop they had released prisoners to clear the platform.

It was now almost Easter and what seemed like a lifetime had passed since the Allied surrender had taken place in the Ford Company car park, near to Changi prison. All the lead officers had been taken from the camp and not seen again. Rumours circulated and said they had been shot, or taken back to Japan to face humiliation or death, so much for the trophies of war. From being left to fend for themselves at Changi and Selarang the Japanese Officers had suddenly introduced a new punitive regime. Beatings increased. Initially such venomous attacks were reserved for Malays and Tamils, though Chinese had always been brutally beaten on sight. It was hard to believe that onl;y four months ago he was celebrating in the Happy World on Lavender Road in Singapore with his San Miguel beer. The night before, he had frequented the New World dance hall full of slim, beautiful Malaysian girls all looking for a European husband even an Irish one. He remembered he had planned to go to the Great World the night after, but he never made it. His world, the Great World had crumbled to dust under the Japanese bombardment. As Owen looked around ,the possibility of death was now imminent. It would be a slow death, not the quick promise of death that war in the trenches would bring. They were now lice-ridden; beginning to starve; some half-naked; a few barefoot. It could only get worse. He fingered the rosary in his pocket, wondering what journey had God planned for him. And then found himself saying God what God! They had been herded into the steel cattle trucks at Singapore Railway station

170

some three days ago. The journey was slow and laborious; often stopping in sidings to take on wood, or to strafe the surrounding woodland of any possible retaliation from local Malay or Chinese kampongs. For large parts of the country, especially as they moved further north, the woodland gave way to increasingly larger tracks of impenetrable rainforest. Escape sometimes crossed Owen's mind. After a brief resistance at Changi, the officers having refused to sign a no escape agreement, they eventually relented after several bad beatings. Looking out of his spy hole he wondered why the clamour to escape. After all, where would you go and how would you get there? For a moment he remembered being in Connor's cellar watching and waiting for the Republicans to turn up.

So far the Japs had only allowed two stops when all six hundred men on board had been able to stretch their legs. Both stops were in tracks of virgin jungle. Many men grabbed leaves and foliage for use at both ends of a human's dietary system. Some grabbed flower blossom as it gave them something to smell and wonder at. Man doesn't live by bread alone, thought Owen. The temperature in the carriage was now dropping as the train rose higher through the Cameroon Highlands.

"Do you think there's a possibility of going to Penang? Jim."

"Not sure. If the train starts cutting east. Maybe so. But why?" He spoke slowly with short shallow breaths. At Changi they had initially been put to work clearing warehouses and loading merchandise on to Japanese lorries, but after this a different pattern of working had been established. The Japs had somehow accessed their army records and the men had been divided into assigned groups. From what could be gathered from observations and local intelligence each group would be dropped off at different points along the way. So far no-one had been dropped off, only the dead.

The train suddenly slowed and the braking systems clanked into action bringing the train to a grinding halt some two hundred yard further on. The carriage was disturbingly quiet. High pitched voices broke the air. "Speedo! Speedo!" Two rifle butts thudded on the doors. The carriage doors opened and the blinding white light of day entered the steel cattle truck. Jim whispered to Owen. "Kempetai." Two Japanese military officers, the Japanese Gestapo, wandered along the siding track. They stopped and scanned each truck. The first pointed to an injured Chinese in their carriage and called out to the two guards "Ichi speedo." There's one. The second spotted another, injured Tamil native. "Ni speedo." That's two quick. The injured Tamil was dragged so violently out of the truck that he almost tumbled down the eighty foot drop that formed the cliff edge of the siding some fifty yards away. An Australian grabbed the Tamil's free arm and broke his fall but got a rifle butt in his back for his trouble. The two Asians were lined up with around twenty other injured travelers and herded towards the back of the train. Jim nudged Owen, "The tracks are heading north".

"So we're heading to Thailand. Ban Pong is the next big station."

The group of injured Tamils and Chinese having staggered and stumbled by them had been lined up on the edge of the siding. They looked with imploring eyes

172

at their POW captives, knowing in their hearts what was about to happen. Knowing that no-one could change it. Some began to whimper in high pitched voices as if praying for help from an imaginary god. But none came. Within minutes a small squad of Japanese carrying machine guns came and stood in a short, threatening line. Before anyone could raise their voice in protest firing commenced, and all twenty fell like fallen trees. One Tamil still moved. A Jap soldier walked over to him took out his parang and in a downward movement struck twice, crushing his skull and the remaining seconds of life out of him. The Japanese soldiers then proceeded to drag each of the bodies towards the siding's ravine, and threw them one by one over the edge. They sailed like flailing dolls into the void and landed some one hundred feet below. One of the kempetai officers, Captain Sato, addressed the trucks through a wooden loud hailer. His voice echoed up the mountain side. In broken "Japlish", somewhere between Japanese and English he shouted, "Let this be lesson! No escapee! No work! No eat!"He walked alongside the trucks repeating to each carriage in turn. As he passed, the carriage doors on each truck were slammed shut. With the carriage doors now shut, the train moved out of the siding heading north to Ban Pong and everlasting servitude.

Jim exhaled a loud breath. Owen rested his arm on the carriage door, all the energy had drained from him. He knew that he and Jim were having the same thoughts; their captivity had taken a new turn. They would have to fight a different war. He still couldn't believe the speed of the Japanese conquest. No sooner had they attacked Pearl Harbour and on the following day they landed in

173

Malaya. He thought again the following day. Harder to take in was the sinking of HMS Repulse and HMS Prince of Wales the day after. It was all so quick and final. The rules had changed. The sanctuary, he had momentarily found in the army had now been brushed aside. Yet he still lived and cherished the thoughts of his mother, Matt, his sister and Connor and always Marion. The murder of the Asian civilians lingered in his and other's minds, until they were subsumed under other gross and subsequent atrocities. Any feelings of security were now gone. Owen tried to quell his inner fears. The train rolled on through the vivid green and mud of the rice padi meadows; passing miles of neatly planted rubber trees, palm oil trees and groves of banana trees. Mingling quietly through the carriage, Squadron Leader Aidan Tierney, the squadron doctor, carrying a bag of broken coconut and pieces of banana, water and aspirins to hand out. He took the pulse of many soldiers and checked Jim McCabe's heart. As the train entered Nong Pladuk station, two, new, pristine Japanese steam engines fully stoked up and ready to go came into view. Both had been delivered days before from Japan to Ban Pong. Having lived in a world of half-verified truths, the rumours that had begun to circulate, that they would be part of some vast grandiose scheme, now became clear to all. They were here to build a railway. The rumours ended in Nong Pladuk and the nightmare was just beginning.

Stiff from sleeplessness, Owen helped Jim down on to the track. The internees sat in mixed groups like swarms of bees, tired swarthy men dozing on each other's shoulders. Some coughed, some retched, some smoked, some stared but few spoke. The rising level of humidity had sucked the strength out of them, like a spider on a freshly caught fly. Owen's eyes sank to his meal a cup of luke-warm rice. He picked out the weevils and with resignation ate the remaining rice. The days that followed strangely took on a common routine. Each morning the military captives, British, Australians, Americans alongside civilian Chinese, Malays and Thais, were divided into groups and marched out of the makeshift camp. A small team always remained to continue building the camp shelters hurriedly erected in the days before. Some teams carried wicker baskets and chunkels, bamboo hoes, for the collecting and carrying of dirt to create the sixty foot embankments along the line. For the terrain was difficult. A hotchpotch of hills and valleys, created the constant need to build viaducts and bridges, or high steeped embankments of earth to bear the rails of the new carriageway to Burma. Owen because of his skills using a theodolite (the result of a one week course) had been placed in a group whose task it was to lay out the new markers that plotted the route of the new railway. In this group were two other Irish men, one from Tipperary and one from Ulster and Jim McCabe.

Soon, each morning began with the ear-splitting Japanese bugle call which reverberated across the camp. Quickly the days filled with the sounds of cutting bamboo; sledgehammers rattling across the valley; the grunts of near naked prisoners, in blistering heat, carrying immense wooden sleepers; falling trees; and the interminable shouts and screams of prisoners in pain followed by the mocking scornful laughter of the guards.

The day was punctuated with two moments to eat a small mug or bowl of weevil infested rice. Today Owen's rice was served in a bowl that had previously contained Yardley soap. He quickly drew breath realizing how long it had been since he'd had a decent shave.

Days passed. Weeks passed. Months went by. The iron rails grew longer heading increasingly northward, through Kanchanaburi, Prankasi, Chunkai and now Tha Kilen, overstretching the supply of water, fuel and food. Conditions in camp worsened the further north they travelled. There was always a buzz in the camp when Red Cross packages arrived. Even the guards relaxed. Owen had forgotten how soft a handkerchief could be and savoured the freshness of a mouth full of toothpaste. He cherished for two weeks the small pot of marmite that provided a thunder-burst of taste in the world of bland, luke-warm rice. A full stomach fosters hope of survival, even escape. But as the days wore on Qwen was brought face to face with his own mortal end. Hunger was draining the strength from him and the will to survive. He had risen that morning in anxiety, his mind full of hopeless thoughts. Will I die today? Will I never say goodbye to my mother? Will I ever see Marion again? Will I never understand what my father wanted for me? God give me time. He murmured under his breath. He was one of a party of six sent to check the markers leading through the foothills to the Wampo trestle viaduct. Jim and the two Irish men fell in behind the two guards and Owen. It may have been Owen's restrained response or the dullness in Owen's eyes that Jim noticed that made him place a hand on Owen's shoulder and said ,"Stay focused Owen." Owen shrugged

176

but could not answer. Though they did not walk far from base camp Owen wilted under the steep climb up the side of the valley. With nothing to block his view, the vastness of the rainforest hit him. It rolled out before him like an endless sea of green impenetrable forest. No roads, no tracks, no refuge from death by capture, death by bandits or death by starvation. For a moment his chest became tight with fear and hot tears fell across his face. He wiped his face quickly. Jim came across. "Bad day Owen?"

"No escape Jim! Where would you go? We are beyond finding!" Owen blurted out glancing across the valley. "We are going to die here!"

"Owen look at me." Owen looked up.

"Don't hope too much. Hope will kill you he murmured in his head. Keep busy. Don't do too little. Stay focused on what's at hand. You can either fight or flight. And as flight is impossible, unless you've grown wings on all that lovely rice Nippon has fed you." Owen half-laughed and smiled momentarily that morning. "We have to fight to tell the story." The Korean guard moved to split them up, nudging Owen in the back with the muzzle of his rifle. They set about checking the markers for the rail track. In the past they had fiddled with marker locations so that the track went off course and had to be rebuilt, delaying completion of the track and hindering the Japanese war effort. Initially when this happened the survey team was given a beating. Sometimes even the guards or the Japanese surveyors were beaten, having allowed it to happen. But subterfuge was increasingly difficult to set up and severe beatings increased. Today the team was too tired to move markers. They made their way down the slope. All six, even the guards were breathing hard as the descent became more treacherous. A fallen tree that had been easily crossed on the way up, now presented a major barrier going down. Just as Owen negotiated the lowest branch he stumbled, but the guard who was following thought he was trying to escape and gave a sudden twist, bringing the muzzle of his rifle square across Owen's back. He tumbled like a bowling ball, squeezing unerringly between two huge boulders and lay dazed but out of sight of the two guards at the foot of a large baobab tree. The guards went berserk, pushing Jim down the slope, "Speedo! Speedo!" Both were unwilling to pursue Owen themselves. Owen half-opened his eyes to find his legs caught up in the roots of the tree. He tried to scramble to his feet despite the searing pain in his shoulder when his hand touched something soft and warm. His immediate reaction was to withdraw his hand but was surprised and elated to see a plump, red, ripe watermelon, the size of a small football resting against the back of the large boulder. His senses returned. He rapidly looked around and realized all five melons, could not be seen from the hill top. Suddenly he was overtaken by emotion he plunged his teeth into the melon, filled with the dread of discovery and an even greater dread of not being able to eat every life-giving morsel. In this moment he didn't care if this was his last meal. Despite his hunger the morsels would not go down quick enough. Melon spilling from his mouth was retrieved in his fingers. The dread of discovery and some inner feeling to restrain his feelings he consumed half of the melon. Then wiping his mouth and what clothes , he tucked another large melon into the ragged remains of his shirt and holding his arm across his body pretending he was hurt he began the ascent up through the two boulders. "Sorry! Sorry! Go-men-nasai! Go-men-nasai!" He screamed. Jim appeared from the other side. "Owen! Thank God! Are you hurt?"

"No. Bruised not broken!" he said with a smile on his face.

"And the arm?"

Owen moved the torn flap of his shirt back and let Jim glimpse the melon.

"Jesus loves us." Jim immediately took off his threadbare over jacket and placed it round Owen's shoulders disguising the enlarged shape of Owen's chest. They began together to mount the steep slope with renewed vigour. They edged slowly up to where the Japanese guards waited."Go-men-nasai! Ari-gar-to!" uttered Owen, nodding and bowing as he said it.

"Shi-ma-su," (Get on) said one guard

"In-sog-in-nasai," (Hurry up)

"Wa-kar- im-masai," (Don't understand) replied Owen.

The guards both gave Jim and Owen a heavy prod with their rifles.

"Hai! Hai!" both Owen and Jim said in unison.

By sheer good luck they succeeded in returning to camp without discovery. After a quick and simple feast the four made plans to return that night and claim the hidden bounty. Leaving camp was easy. No fences and few lights created few concerns about slipping away. Getting back in was the problem. In some camps prisoners were free to ramble and often came across Thai settlements to barter for food. Leaving at night in this camp was full of dangers. Not only was it punishable with death, but also no-one wanted to spend a night in the jungle. The heavy swarms of mosquitoes became unbearable after dark. All four wore improvised head gear made from old mosquito nets. They looked like four bizarre bee keepers as they followed the fragile bamboo fence that ran around the whole camp. The guard room stood to the right of the main entrance and often one isolated, bored guard stood on the far side of the camp, a few hundred metres from the rail track. To the east side of camp, away from the prevailing winds, a row of latrine trenches with planks across were always left unguarded and offered a way into the jungle without being discovered. The four edged their way, from shadow to shadow into the locomotive yard, passing the water tower and huge firewood dump to stand on the planks leading to the latrines. The smell was unbearable and all felt the pressure to control their desire to retch. Beyond the range of the weak oil and paraffin lights, and the occasional light powered off a petrol generator, the light diminished rapidly once they entered the rainforest canopy. Jim gestured with his hand to follow a path of broken branches that he had marked out, returning earlier that day. As he walked he carefully broke more. The rushing sound made by the hordes of Cicadas in the trees and the screams and barks emanating from the forest masked any noise they made. Once they came to the river they followed it down more easily, and soon came to the small track leading up to the two boulders. The moonlight flashed across the river, as it moved rapidly downstream. They moved up hill quickly urged on by their anticipation of the reward ahead. Soon they all stood together for a moment feasting their eyes on the grove of ripe melons. Looking around again they checked they were alone. They had brought two well worn blankets to carry home their treasure. There were six melons of varying sizes. Their desire to eat them where they lay –to quell their rising desires was too strong so they quartered the largest and had their fill.

The journey back was fraught with difficulties. The light had diminished even more and a light drizzle had begun to fall. On a night like this back in camp a thousand mugs, containers and groundsheets would be placed in the open to catch the falling nectar of rain. They all licked their lips and rubbed the rain into their faces. As they neared the locomotive yard the guard, for some unknown reason, decided to set off on a walk towards the water tower. He was heading in their direction, immediately they ducked back into the shadow behind the large firewood dump, some twenty foot high. As he maneuvered around the east side the foursome edged around the west side. The guard, then, stopping while he found a decent seat on one of the larger tree trunks, took out a cigarette. Sweat trickled down Jim McCabe's cheek as he tried hard not to swat the increasing swarm of mosquitoes around his face. An hour passed. Owen signaled he was moving forward and edged around the firewood dump careful, noting where he was treading. To his horror walking towards him was a new Japanese Officer he had never seen before. He leant back into the shadow and pulled a small branch in front of him. As long as he remained still he would not be seen. The Officer made his way around the other side and within seconds a barrage of thuds, thumps and screams pierced the air. The guard suddenly fell forward into the open, stumbling and rising, as the officer kicked his butt over and over again. "No sleep on duty!"

"Go-men nasai," he screamed over and over. He fell flat on his face within metres of Owen's feet. If the guard rose up now he would see Owen. But another wayward boot persuaded him to crawl as quickly as he could away. The danger passed as if it had never occurred and the four returned to the quiet of their hut. Many went to sleep that night on a fuller stomach than the previous night but as always the night brought renewed terrors.

As the darkness blackened and sleep invaded Owen's body the night began to fill up again, as it always did, with half-imagined buildings and distant voices. He drifted and surged, sinking his teeth into melon after melon-but they weren't melons they were apples, an apple his mother slipped into his pocket the night he ran to save Matt. He ran and ran, over the sea pinks, into the rainforest until he came to the Happy World full of hysterical Thai girls pulling him in, with dragon gargoyles leering out from under the eaves. A swarm of Buddhist monks in yellow robes uttering guttural prayers, droned like bees, smothering him with incense. Black and tan butterflies flew from their mouths, settling into his eyes and on his lips. They wanted to know his secrets and he lurched struggling to sweep them away. He had a terrible weight on his back, it pushed him down. He ran on into the night slipping into the Happy World and the Great World and then stood alone in The Union jack Club. His father appeared, knocking at the window but not able to come in. His mother stood, clothed in an orange light at the bottom of his bed. Standing by her the priest and Connor. Connor was carrying something on his shoulder. It was Joe with a bullet in his head. But something made him look closer. There was a bulge under Connor's jacket. Connor was carrying a gun. Owen tried to cry out but his voice was muffled. "Connor? Connor? What's going on?" he screamed but no sound came.

The priest is laughing. "Don't you know?" Your father made a covenant with God. Owen screamed and woke up. He woke in darkness and sweat, a cold sweat, fear lingered in his body and he had to sit up and put his feet on the ground and he cried because he knew the weight on his shoulders was Matt and he couldn't change anything.

The following morning three events would transpire that would change Owen's life forever. He awoke to the sound of torrential rain, the first of spring and the harbinger that the monsoon had arrived. With the coming of the rainy season, cholera also raised its deadly threat. As the monsoon hit full force that day the river swelled quickly carrying debris and branches sometime food down river. Six Tamils had managed to slaughter a python beheading it before it engulfed them. A wash in the river before tenco that morning was impossible. Tenco itself was interrupted by the second shockwave as they gathered together for roll call. A new commandant had been appointed and he made his intentions clear from that moment. He stood before the assembled prisoners, his attitude turning from smiling, to sneering and hostility. Speaking in American English it was clear he had been educated abroad.

"You are vanquished! You are less than the dirt on my boot! You are nothing! From today we make new changes-we make more speed – we work twelve hour days- including sick person. No work! No eat!" His heavy cheeks puffed up as he spat the words out

Aidan attempted to speak."Bug-er-ro! Its madness too many men will die." Two Korean guards immediately ran to silence the interruption, when Sato, the new commandant raising his hand, halted their movement. A sickly smile pervaded his face.

"You are doctor; all men sick or injured will present themselves for work. Only those that work will eat. I hold you responsible for speed of railway."

"We need quinine, inkie if you want men to work."

"You will have quinine when speed of work improves. The railway is behind schedule and men will work twelve hours until we catch up."

The five guards in full battle uniform behind him stood to attention. Sato began to strut like a bantam cock along the wooden verandah of his hut, which led to his nick name of 'Cocky bastard' each day he would , after rising late, have a metal bath, filled with boiling water, placed on the verandah where he would bathe while consuming large quantities of Saki. It quickly became all too clear what the regime would become. For as the dawn light brightened and tenco began, a native woman, who had thrown a fowl to a group of prisoners the day before- had been caught and strung up, on the camp perimeter. The prisoners watched her die slowly as they made their way out of camp that morning. Sadism and cholera had now entered the camp and these two things alone would bring

184

unmitigated hardship to Owen but the third event would change his life.

Aidan turned to Jim and Owen, his face tense with a vision of the future for he knew that death would visit the camp every night and day, every waking and sleeping hour. It would be like the plague taking the first born, the young first and then the old-those whose bodies were not fully formed and those who were no longer at the peak of their powers. He knew that cholera, a water-borne disease would begin to take its toll. Death would follow very quickly from the first symptoms of stomach cramps, through dehydration and eventual kidney failure. No matter how hard he tried no matter how clever his use of makeshift saline drips with bottles and bamboo thorns he would be overwhelmed with death.

With tenco over the men made their way to their new stations. A new camp was being constructed at Touchan South, in Hellfire Pass; each day increasingly more men were brought up from the south. As Owen returned at dusk, the camp was awash with new prisoners. As he came into the light of the camp, a group of men, breathing heavy, carrying wooden boxes full of explosives-sticks of gelignite, after having just completed a four mile hike in the heat of the rainforest, entered the main gates. Something familiar made him focus on a Korean guard beating a prisoner with a pick handle. In the glare of the headlights of a jeep entering the main gates Owen suddenly realized that under the black helmet of hair, Connor's eyes were burning with frustration. Owen immediately began to run shouting,

"Go-men-nasai!" The Korean guard backed off. Connor looked up. Incredulous at first, "Owen is it you."

"What's left of me."

"Thank God." He muttered and Connor collapsed into Owen's arms. When Conner awoke he found himself in the makeshift hospital. He had passed blood in his urine, owing to the pick handle beating he had taken and spent days in the hospital recovering. Aidan Tierney had made sure he had been placed on light duties. This morning, his first return to real work, he was to accompany Owen with two guards to barter and buy food from the local villages south of Hellfire Pass. Up to this point Owen had made little contact. When Owen turned up he found Connor was surprisingly quiet. "Connor?"

Connor lit a cigarette and breathed in deeply. Smoking always reduced his feelings of hunger. His mouth was taut and dry and he shrugged stiffly. For what seemed moments there was an uneasy silence between them.

"Owen," Connor responded with a nod.

"Follow me," said Owen and led him outside onto the jungle perimeter path way. They both were unkempt, haggard, and weary as they made their way through the dense undergrowth together. The tall trees seemed to close in on them as they emerged high up on one of the slopes of the surrounding hills. The minutes of quiet panic continued,both hardly speaking to each other. At the edge of the clearing a lorry stood waiting, with two Japanese, armed guards. In the distance both could hear sporadic rifle and artillery fire. While Owen and Connor clambered into the back of the lorry, the two Japanese guards climbed into the cab. The lorry set off on to a dirt track bearing left on to a wider jungle path, not long constructed. The vehicle lurched and twisted, crashing down heavily, as the stoic driver veered off the road down a pot-holed track leading to a hard –deserted, half hidden village. The soldiers had been before. They knew the route as they sped around corners at break-neck speed. They also knew where they had planned to go and not just to buy food. Connor was in obvious pain but did not cry out. Owen again tried to make conversation, but Connor was evasive in his answers. "When did you join up?"

"A few years back"

"Captured in Singapore?"

"Borneo." Connor responded never taking his eyes from the back of the vehicle. Owen relented, saving the questions about his mother, Liam and Marion, and something else small but annoying at the back of his mind. The lorry clanged to a dead stop with a snort and a shake outside what looked like a massage parlour. The two Japanese soldiers began to giggle like school kids. They took off their gas masks and extra uniform to stand only in their shirt and trousers. Having stripped off they exited the cab leaving their guns and keys in the ignition. Two pretty Thai girls in green brocade jackets came out to greet them and escort them inside. Connor and Owen could not take in what had just happened. Connor suddenly renewed, stood up in the back of the lorry. Jumping down he ran round, climbed in the cab, and rummaged through the glove box and door pockets. Stuffing two half-filled packets of American cigarettes into the pockets of his shorts, he placed his hand on the nearest rifle.

"Don't be stupid. How far do you think we'll get?"Owen interjected. Owen couldn't believe what he was saying. Why not? Shoot the bastard guards and drive off. Escape! Escape! Was he afraid to die? Was he a coward? Here was a golden opportunity. Escape while you can .But other words tumbled out of his mouth. He would not loose Connor. He was a link to the past and a door to the future.

"Far enough." Connor responded.

"We couldn't even find our way back to camp"

"Why leave the rifles?"

"They know. They know."

Connor released the rifle, because he knew too.

"We've little food. No maps and no compass."Connor didn't like having the truth rammed home. "We have to wait. The Japs are losing and will have to retreat soon. We heard the Americans are taking Iwo Jima. Besides I need to go back to Ireland. God willing." Connor relented he knew Owen was right, but he also knew he could not go back to Ireland.

A girl carrying a tray of orange sugared hen's feet, came up smiling muttered, " Hai," and offered them for sale. Connor produced his half packet of American cigarettes. She smiled and nodded, but running off returned with a bag full of bananas in exchange for the full half pack. Connor agreed and while the Japs had their play time they had high tea.

The small moment of hope seemed to relax Connor as if he wanted to confess the burden he was carrying. "I can't go back to Ireland, but added quickly, "You must! You've changed Owen. The army has helped to sort out your life. I can see how Jim and Aidan and the men respect you. Even the protties from Northern Ireland trust you. If you ever get out of this hell hole go back to Ireland. Your name is clear."

"What do you mean Connor?"

"I found your da's walking stick in Chapman's Pool." Owen was startled. "If you had waited one hour more I might have stopped you joining the British Army." Owen took the bull by the horns and asked "What happened that night? Who were all those people and why were you carrying a gun."Connor was now startled. Did Owen know? Connor began again. "Owen you're a far better son than I ever was."Owen blinked. "When our das went to America they were attacked by an anti - Irish protestant group called the Bowery Boys. My da was badly beaten. You father had made good money on the stock market and they wanted the takings. They were in no fit state to defend themselves so my da went in secret to Cana Gael to ask for their protection. The price was to work for Cana Gael and my da agreed. To this day you are the only person, apart from me and my father that knew about this arrangement. Your da on the appointed day made a fortune, no-one is quite sure how, as the market crashed and he never told anyone what he did. One person however did know the truth. When your father went back to Ireland carrying the first shipment of money, my da stayed on to work for Cana Gael. They fell out the night he left. Your dad was tired of seeing the money go to buy guns. He wanted it to go to farmers to pay off their debts and he wanted to build more schools. He wanted you and other Irish lads to get a good education. He had great plans for you," he breathed hard, "You were lucky to have someone who wanted so much

189

for you. He fell in love with your mother but regretted giving up the priest hood. It was as if he had made a covenant with God and then reneged on it. Your mother loved your father very much, but my da said that from the moment she left America, something troubled her. She had a secret but was devastated when your dad died. Her grief made her make mistakes, big mistakes. Joe was no good. She must have thought God was punishing her. Crazy as it seems. Owen wanted to know more, but the small something at the back of his mind need to be expressed. "But why can't you go back to Ireland and why were you carrying a gun that night?"

"Because I dishonoured my father."

"Not you Connor."

"When our fathers fell out, my da continued to work for Cana Gael delivering money to the Brotherhood. He eventually took over the job done by Sean Kenny. My da got drawn in to carrying more and more money, taking bigger risks. Eventually he was caught, just before you left. The Tans had taken to giving him regular beatings and by the time I got to see him he was in a terrible state. He was dying. I had to do something."

Owen began to piece things together. "So how did you come to meet with Joe that night, the night I ran the moor?"Connors eyes looked down as if remembering the events. "I met Joe by accident at O'Leary's farm gate. He was as drunk as hell; he had those frightened eyes and was largely incoherent, but he managed to tell me he had an important meeting to go to. The priest, Father Ryan had arranged the meeting at your mother's farm. They thought the rumours that someone was dying of diphtheria would warn off the Black and Tans."

"But the Tans did visit. So what made them come?"

"I told them," Connor's voice began to break, "God forgive me."

"Why Connor? Why?

"I thought I'd done a deal with the Tans to stop beating my da."

"So what happened?"

"The beatings stopped for a while but then continued. O'Leary was killed that night, for resisting arrest despite the fact he was in jail.. The mausers were found and two other Republicans were arrested. It was a bad night." Connor paused for a moment. "That night I had to hit Joe, one to save you but I needed to get away. The Garda had just called in to say how bad the river was, when you arrived. I knew the Tans were on the way, better that I was'nt there. Eventually the brotherhood found out that it was me who had betrayed them. By then I had already left Ireland. My da will be turning in his grave. God help me!"

"You can't keep kicking yourself. All of us would have made mistakes faced with those difficulties. With God willing and I go back to Ireland, come with me Connor."

"You're too good Owen. Stay alive and when you get back tell your kids I'm sorry."

"Do you know if my da said anything about me becoming a priest?"

"I only know, he regretted not being accepted into the seminary."

"Will you do me a favour Owen? If you get back to Ireland will you place some flowers on my father's grave. Tell him I'm sorry."

"Come with me?"

"I'll not make it. Promise me!"

Owen nodded, "If I make it I will."

Before Owen could ask more, the two Japanese soldiers came out laughing and shouting "Ari-gar-toe."They clambered awkwardly into the cab, the result of too much saki, and began putting on their uniform. Once they were dressed they began to reassert their presence with occasional bouts of laughter. Owen and Connor were ordered to dismount the lorry and to march down the road to a small market stall. Bags of rice were piled up in a squalid outhouse. Both could see the rice had been there for weeks and weeks. Twenty hundredweight bags were purchased, and carried along the road to the lorry. On the way back one of the soldiers rummaged over and over again, looking for something in the glove box and pockets. He became annoyed and frustrated but never guessed that his American cigarettes had been traded for some sugared hen's feet and a bag full of bananas.

On return to the camp the early signs of the new regime being put into place were evident. The sounds of a deep pit, big enough to house a metal framed cage, being dug by two prisoners in the middle of the parade ground, could be heard. It was clear anyone incarcerated in the cage would not be able to sit up or stretch out, while being exposed to the full force of the mid-day sun. With little water or sustenance offered to the incumbent, it was a certain excruciating death. The Japanese guards had already named it the no-good house. Connor an Owen eyed it with concern as they unloaded the bags of rice at the temporary kitchen, erected on site. At the next tenco the first incarceration would take place. Jim and

Aidan wandered across." Owen we need to talk. Not here. Latrines, in ten minutes." After unloading the rice bags, Owen and Connor made their way to the back of the camp and the latrine trenches. It was not a place you would go to if you could at all help it. So it must be urgent thought Owen. Aidan and Jim had already arrived and appeared from behind a small hut. "Over here", Jim whispered forcefully. The four crouched down, concealed behind a huge pile of cut banana leaves used for roofing the huts. Aidan began. "We've discovered there is a four gallon drum of quinine sulphate in the explosives hut at the back of the locomotive yard."Owen turned to Connor and then to Jim."What have you got in mind Aidan?"

Jim answered, "We need to take it tonight. If the rumours are true and the Japs are on the run, retreating will begin soon. Medication like that will save lives."

"Problem if we leave it too late it's likely to be moved."

Jim made a quick tour to check they were still alone and returned to the conversation."Are we up for it?" The four consented they had no alternatives. Cholera was already taking its toll five men had died in the last few days.

As the bugle sounded for the night curfew at the first signs of dusk, the four wearing bandanas, crept along the bamboo fencing heading for the latrines. They took the long way round and eventually stood in the locomotive yard, some two hundred yards from the explosives hut. Usually the hut was guarded but the loss of two soldiers to cholera meant that they were overstretched. Jim and Aidan had brought two stolen knives. Some fifty yards of open land lay between them and the back of the hut. A small roving spotlight operated by a guard on a platform nesting in a nearby tree, flashed across the area every ten to fifteen minutes. The hut looked impregnable, but Jim had spotted a weakness in the lower roof some days before. Connor offered to go first. Owen suddenly felt the danger of the moment, "Take care Connor." He whispered. Crawling on all fours he slid along the ground to the back of the hut evading the roving spotlight. He could reach the wooden slats holding the banana leaves in place. Within a short time he had made a hole big enough for a man to slip through. Jim and Owen ran across and Connor and Jim manhandled Owen through the hole. It was a slick operation. Within minutes despite the poor light Owen had found the four gallon drum. Slipping the knife into the poorly secure lock, he managed to open the door of the hut. He had to, as the weight of the drum was too heavy to lift through the gaping hole in the roof. Even so in his weakened state it was a trial to drag to the door. As he began to inch the door slowly open, something, the diffusion of light or the sound of boots scraping on soil, made him stop in his tracks. Aidan's cuckoo whistle confirmed his thoughts. They were in danger. Outside the hut the three watched in horror as two guards were making a random check on the grounds. As yet they had not realized that anything was out of place, but if they came closer all hell would break loose. Connor sensed the danger first and without hesitation ran off into the rainforest, making enough noise to wake the dead and attract the guard's attention who duly followed, raising the alarm as they did. Jim and Aidan acted quickly retrieving Owen and the drum from the hut and moving in the direction of the latrines and safety. As they entered their hut they could see no sight of Connor, but all hell had broken loose as the grounds of the camp were flooded with extra guards. Within ten minutes a bugle call summoned all prisoners to take tenco. The Cocky Bastard strutted across the verandah and began to spell out the consequences of the night's excitement. Owen stood still but his eyes were everywhere looking for Connor. Connor had still not surfaced.

"A drum of quinine has been stolen and I want the persons responsible and the drum back. We will reassemble in ten minutes to give you time to give up the perpetrators and the drum. Be assured without the return, retribution will follow."Aidan threw a glance at Jim, who shook his head. Still, there was no sign of Connor. After discussion the senior officers decided to do nothing as either way a lot of people would get beaten. Needless to say the Cocky Bastard was angry, with no drum of quinine returned. He clicked his fingers at the two Japanese soldiers who entered the hut and dragged out Connor's half-conscious body on to the verandah. He had been badly beaten. "This man was found breaking the curfew. He has something to do with the quinine, but has refused to say who is involved." An instantaneous round of applause rippled around the assembled men."Be quiet!" Cocky Bastard screamed in frustration. The guards ran in and began beating any one clapping with bamboo sticks. The applause subsided but it had already marked the first note of defiance. "This man will be first in no-good house." Connor was immediately man handled into the man –made cage, crying out in obvious pain. "He will stay there until the drum is returned."

The morning sun rose with a vengeance. Connor had stirred and adjusted his position as best he could, to find the coolest part of his cage. But soon he would have no refuge. Jim and Owen had been in deep discussion about how to get him water and pain killers but at present no strategy had materialised. Time was ticking. Within a few short hours the sun had risen steeply in the sky and the cage was increasing exposed to its brutal effects. Connor began to cry out. A bugle call sounded the start of tenco and the prisoners assembled in front of the no-good house. "Save your friend." Cocky Bastard implored smiling through his teeth. Connor shouted in a surprisingly resilient voice, "Tell him to ." But two guards immediately prodded him with bamboo sticks stifled his response. Although his cries subsided he was no less defiant. Tenco was dismissed and the prisoners set to work. But new rumours that Iwo Jima had been taken by the Americans had circled the camp, and raised expectations of release and increased defiance. As the men returned before dusk, they were greeted by Connor singing 'When Irish eyes are smiling' in a low, broken voice. Though he continued to fight, it was clear to all, he wouldn't last another day.

Dusk succumbed to intense darkness and only the oil lamps sprayed a thin veil of light across the open square. Then something strange happened, something that had waited all day, something that no-one queried. One grows tired of looking for reason or subterfuge in all that happens but when whispers ran around the camp that the Japs were handing out a ration of saki to all, no-one refused the sustenance nor asked why. The saki had its effect, an air of jollity engulfed the camp, for a moment even laughter, even Cocky Bastard seemed a shade lighter. But soon the camp grew silent and sleep had overtaken the inmates. Even Owen slept, his body cried out for eons of deep sleep, and whether he liked it or not the saki had erased all of his fears of living or dying and any concerns about Connor. This was something he would regret in the morning.

The morning came in bright, burning sunlight. Owen awoke with a start, his head ached, and his sixth sense kicked in straight away, something didn't feel right. It was too quiet. There had been no bugle call. It suddenly struck him the camp had overslept. "The camp is too quiet?" he murmured. Rising quickly from the bed he stretched out and roused Jim McCabe a few feet away. Jim awoke with a startled cry. Looking round he realised something was up. "What's going on Owen?"
"I don't know Jim the camp's too quiet. No bugle call."
They dressed quickly in what clothing they were still able to wear, slipping on boots and shorts and they peered out across the assembly ground. "There are no Japs on duty."Owen could hardly believe what he was saying. "Jim there are no guards on the gate." Owen tried hard to comprehend what was happening. "Let's just check." said Jim in a steady voice. They scampered across the assembly ground like children playing hide and seek, keeping to the shadows and looking for cover. "The Japs have gone," circulated round and round in his mind like a windmill, when another thought struck him "Where's Connor?" From every available vantage point , no guards, no Koreans were seen, the gates were open and two abandoned jeeps were rudely parked across the

entrance to the food store, starkly confirmed the Japs had left in the night. Owen returned to Jim stood in the doorway of the makeshift hospital. "The Japs have gone." Jim looked blank faced and repeated, "The Japs have gone." And then quite unexpectedly they grabbed each other and danced round in a circle hysterical with laughter. Jim brought them back to reality. "Owen, get two men check the food store, get those two vehicles up and running , but first find Connor." Jim went to wake the rest of the men and particularly to get the radio corporal to make contact with the outside world. Suddenly there was a buzz and the captives worked with renewed hope. The food store gave up eight bags of weevil infested rice which once cleaned was edible. A foraging party was sent out to find what food the forest would give up. But no sign of Connor raised fears the Japs had taken him with them. A wider search was organised. Two hours later two bodies were found under a tarpaulin at the back of the makeshift hospital, one was dead the other barely alive. Aidan Turner attended. "Well he's dead," pointing to Cocky Bastard. "He has three bayonet wounds in his chest, but Connor is still alive. " He administered one of the few shots of morphine left.Connor opened his eyes. "Connor thank God," Owen blurted out. Owen knew by the look Aidan gave him that Connor had not long to live. He also knew that Connor's eyes were asking for him to hear his last rites. Owen was thrown into turmoil, he almost answered he couldn't , but merely nodded his head and clasped his lifeless hands. Almost intuitively he whispered in nomine Patris, et Fillii , Spiritus Sancti, and fingered his rosary in his only remaining pocket, alongside the letter from his mother."Let me hear your confession," Owen continued in a quiet voice. At this prompt Aidan led the onlookers away. In a weak voice Connor , no longer the mountain, tried to catch his breath, recounted in halting exhalations the help he had given to the Black and Tans that led to the imprisonment and death of Sean O'Leary. Owen listened without judging and tried to calm Connor's breathing. "No there's more," and forcefully pressed on. Time was running out and he knew it. "Forgive your mother, " he voice rasped. "She did a terrible thing and thinks God is punishing her for it."Owen's heart jumped." Connor what do you mean?" "I mean forgive her and keep your promise." "Forgive her for what." In the moment Owen said "I will." Connor rasped , " Keep your promise." and his eyes rolled and he slipped away. Owen with tears on his face murmured this is the ,"Lamb of God who takes away all the sins of the world," and with that began to wrap his body in the sheet from his bed. The foraging party returned with summer fruits , a few bananas, and some edible leaves. Food was in short supply, luckily a torrential downpour the following day helped solve the water crisis. With one of the jeeps up and running, and contact made with the outside world, supplies were dropped four days later. Owen knew rescue was ahead. Before they could take their leave of the camp, twenty - eight bodies needed to be buried. Six weak and frail soldiers including Owen, some of the few able- bodied men, had been assigned to burial duty. While it had been possible previously to bury like with like Catholic with Catholic , Protestant with Protestant, Australian with

Australian, Thai with Thai, Japanese with Japanese, the six were overwhelmed with the task ahead. With much arguing about what was right ,what was wrong the sheer physical demand of the task led them to bury all twenty -eight corpses into one shallow grave. Owen said a few words asking forgiveness, in that Captor and Captive now lay together, and hoped that what they could not reconcile in life they could now reconcile in death.

The last sign of rescue was complete, some ten days after the Japs had left, when an American Jeep entered camp and was greeted by two hundred half-naked and starving guys. All he could say was, "Anyone for chocolate". But Owen's thoughts were now on getting back to Ireland to see his mother. God keep her safe. But more was to unravel before he would see home again.

Chapter 8

The Montfort Hospital Ottawa, Canada September 1945

'Clothe the grass of the field'

Owen lay asleep, it was a deep sleep, a restful sleep and a flurry of dreams and memories danced in his eyes. He teetered on the brink as his body released the anxiety of incarceration and he slept relaxed in the knowledge that he would awake for the first time amongst friends. Those in the room waited in anticipation of meeting again; and for some the excitement of meeting for the first time. Outside it was snowing and the falling flakes softened the noise of the city's traffic and landed silently like leaves in a Galtee meadow. Like the snow he softened and drifted, softened and drifted. It was smooth and gentle and yet, and yet it beckoned him to wake. He stirred at the soft caress of his resting hands. Half-waking, half -craving sleep he stirred again, his eyes flickered open, hardly recognising the shapes and shadows of the room. He awoke as if in a dream, as if time had stood still, as if his brother still lived and he had time to make it right."Owen. Owen." A familiar voice, an Irish voice pierced his sleeping consciousness. He awoke in amazement as he gazed upon the youthful, rounded face. His eyes told him this was the mother of his youth, yet his head told him he was still dreaming, but his heart cried out, "Muther. Muther, "as he reached out in desperation to clasp her outstretched hands. Somebody called out into the small ante room close by, "Nurse he's waking up."

As his eyes cleared, his senses told him that the hands and face were not apparitions, but real. But still he could not take it in; he was lost in a void. "Who? Who?" Owen confused in his thoughts, stuttering the words like a young child. "Owen I'm Megan, your ma's sister. Really pleased to meet you," and she took his hand in a warm embrace. "Megan, my Aunt Megan?" They had never met and his mother had only spoken about Megan when a few letters had arrived each Christmas. His eyes wandered over her face again, so like my mother he thought. His eyes turned to the other faces but before he could ask more questions, a grey haired, stooping, older man, in an equally grey suit, stepped forward. "Shalom Owen, I am Gunter and this is Anya my wife, " he said in an Eastern European dialect, still vibrant even after all the time that had passed. Beside him, very well dressed, sat a grey-haired lady with bright, shiny eyes. As he looked towards Gunter, he became aware of the two parallel rows of beds lining each side of the ward. The room bustled with constant activity. War had changed hospital life for good and had now saved more lives than ever. A new, more efficient professionalism was growing which minimised incompetent surgery and reduced infections. Arrangements were in the process of getting the lunch ready. Food was still rationed. Canada had been in a state of emergency since 1939. Dessert would be semolina, better known as 'three six five,' always lamentably available. He suddenly realised who Gunter was," Didn't you give shelter and food to my father and mother when they first came to America."

"We did, but he gave us so much more." Gunter responded with a benevolent grin. Just then Jim McCabe entered on crutches, followed by Marion. "Jim! Marion!" He was shocked to see both but especially Marion. His eyes brightened. He hadn't seen Marion since Malta. How had she got here? How did she know? Marion immediately came over. He held onto Megan's hand and extended his other to Marion. She bent forward and pulled him close, sensing how fragile still he was, and kissed his lips. Emotion overwhelmed him and tears filled his eyes, "It's wonderful to see you." He said in a buoyant but low rasping voice.

"You had us all worried; you've been delirious for weeks, the malaria had such a terrible hold, we thought you might not make it."

"I had you to come back to."

"Yes I have been hoping and waiting my darlin'. I was posted here, just before you arrived courtesy of the Canadian rescue ships, to oversee the care of prisoners captured by the Japanese. I knew if you were alive you would have to pass through here sooner or later. We'll talk when you are stronger." Marion looked round as a young nurse handed her a fileOf patient medical papers. "Right now we need to give you some time to sleep,

Megan and Gunter and Anya have promised to return tomorrow, they have much to tell you."Owen could feel the wave of tiredness sweep through his body, but his mind was now full of excitement and questions. Questions that might be answered and answers that might unlock doors. What stories would they tell him and what would it all mean? Jim placed a gentle hand on his shoulder, "Good to see you back in the land of the living old buddy."

"Jim what happened at the end. I have vague memories of how we got here or even where I am." Jim continued even though Marion silently beckoned him to come away.

"The Americans liberated the camp after Connor died. Old Cocky Bastard was killed by his own troops, seems they did like him either. We were then shipped off to Canada. We landed in New York and came to Ottawa overland by ambulance train. By the way Marion found Gunter, Anya and Megan and made arrangements for them to stay. She is one hell of a lady."

Owen nodded as he watched her walk away realising her long hair was now tied in a bob.

"This place has been set up for us courtesy of the Canadian Government; Marion was posted here because of her talent and skills." Owen noticed the affection in his voice.

"Did we bury Connor before we left?"

"Yes you did and you heard his final words." Jim did not say it was a mass grave. That was something for later.

"I did, didn't I?" Owen wondered as if he had only dreamt it. And then for a moment he couldn't conceive of a world without Connor. "The Japs surrendered shortly after we boarded Carpathian, the ship that brought us here. And the war's over in Europe. Owen responded," That's good."

But Jim added, "It took the dropping of two atom bombs on Hiroshima and Nagasaki to persuade them what to do." Jim shook his head, "Imagine a hundred thousand people dead within the blinking of an eye." Owen couldn't imagine the horror of such devastation, no-one could. He had so much he needed to know especially about his mother. He must get back to Ireland the urgency of his thoughts overwhelmed him. Marion passed by a second later smiled and finally persuaded Jim to hobble off into the next ward. He couldn't take his eyes off Marion noticing the lightness of her walk, as if he was beginning to know her anew. He shouted to Jim, "What's happened to the leg?"

"No sea legs." Owen repeated the words in his mind; amazing he survives incarceration and hand to hand fighting and slips over, on board his rescue ship.

As darkness fell, lights were dimmed in the hospital ward and Marion making her final round of the day stopped at Owen's bed. She was pushing a medicine trolley laden with glass syringes, needles, hand-cut gauze swabs and an assortment of pill bottles and small boxes.

"I need to give you your final antibiotic injection." Owen could not remember having any other injections and queried the dose. "We've been trialling a new antibiotic line called penicillin. It's the new wonder drug. It has had a major impact on recovery time." Marion added, after a short pause wondering if this was the best time to bring it up." I had a conversation with your ma before I left to come here. She gave me a package to give you once you return to Ireland that was the condition she placed on the package, that you return to Ireland." She didn't say that his mother was not in the best of health. "Marion you have been terribly kind can you tell me anything more."

"We can talk later; right now you need rest and the sooner the better." Owen, though his mind was full of anticipation, had to admit she was right and gave in without a fight. With the injection over Marion made her way through the ward stopping at a Belfast sink to wash her hands. She sat down at her desk to plan the monthly cleaning day of the ward, which meant moving beds, lockers, sand screens and sterilising bed pans.

Owen awoke later the following morning to cleaning mayhem. Everyone had been moved. Cleaning was in full swing when Megan, Gunter and Anya, who had been granted special visiting times, walked in. Owen greeted each in turn. Megan was the first to speak. She began to tell Owen the story of how they had met his father on the boat , Lucania and how her sister began to feel about his father as the journey went on. The Five Points was not an easy place to live, often dangerous, rarely generous and sometimes surprising. She recounted their good luck in finding Gunter and Anya in the Five Points. Then she began to tell about the day the robbery took place on board the Lucania, and only she, Megan knew the real answer. Owen reflected on what little he knew about Megan. He remembered the letters arriving at Christmas, containing a postal order to buy presents with, always very generous, and always gratefully received when his father was alive. The letters stopped once his mother married Joe so the money could not go on drinking.

"Your mother loved your father with every beat of her heart. I was there when they first met, something happened, something wonderful. Your father had many talents. They prospered but unfortunately this drew them to the notice of Cana Gael, who made your father a deal just after Liam was beaten." Owen nodded partly knowing the story but still not taking it all in. Where was the story leading? "Remember that your mother had fallen in love with your father, because she then did something she has regretted all of the days of her life." As she answered she placed an old envelope, with a faded heraldic, papal, stamp across the unopened seal, addressed to the Right Reverend John Levine, into his hands. At that moment Marion entered the ward. "It's yours to open." Megan continued. For moments Owen read the address on the front of the envelope, written in his father's hand, when Marion handed him a pair of small scissors. Owen cut through the seal and unfolded the letter inside. He read in silence for a few minutes before saying in surprise, "This is my father's letter of Introduction. How have you got hold of it?" Megan hesitated. Then it dawned on Owen it was his mother who took the letter, having seen it lying on the iron bed.

Megan continued,"Your mother gave it to me, before she and your father left to go to Ireland. She had fallen in love and couldn't bear to lose him. Your father never knew. It was after your father died that the guilt resurfaced believing that she had broken the covenant between your father and God and that your father's untimely death was her punishment. God had taken back what was his. It grew worse because when Matt died she still feared that everything she loved would be taken so she kept you safe by distancing herself from you. "Owen knew in that instant how much he loved his mother, memories flooded back and how much he needed to hold her."I need to see her. I must get back to Ireland." He said in a determined voice.

"Not yet, not until you are well enough to travel that distance, and I shall take you." interrupted Marion.

Gunter spoke," Your father was a fine man. I, we," looking at Anya," miss him greatly. He loved your mother and would have forgiven her, no question about it. I have two gifts, one is something which may help you understand how your father made his money on that fateful day when the market crashed, and the other you have to read for yourself."

From a small handmade rucksack, worn at the buckles, but beautifully preserved, bearing the initials E.D., Gunter took a piece of paper, curled at the edges, a ticket headed Kentucky Derby and a wager note with the words Pink Star and betting odds fifteen to one scrawled over it. Owen poured over it, "So my dad switched the money

208

to Pink Star and put his trust in the Almighty. What would be would be."

"Please take it." Handing Owen the rucksack, "it was something he brought from Ireland. Two nurses wearing white aprons and pink shoulder cloaks glanced across as Owen took the rucksack. "The other piece of the jigsaw is still a mystery and Gunter handed him another unopened envelope bearing the papal seal of St Joseph's College "I have wondered what the judgement was for the last forty years but it was not mine to open. I think you are the one to do it."

Owen took the envelope, and immediately had misgivings about opening it; he felt a pang about leaving it alone for ever. Would it be a Pandora's Box? Something compelled him to open it, the knowledge from which would affect him forever. He carefully prized the letter open and took out the headed notepaper from The Right Reverend John Levine and read. The words began, 'We are pleased to offer you a place'. Owen had not anticipated the answer that his father would have been accepted into the College. He felt he had just been hit with a cannon ball. How will I tell her? Gunter and Anya were visibly pleased, "I think despite all his worldly skills he wanted to become a priest and this was his calling." Gunter added.

Marion had finished her ward round and joined the group. Owen noted how all the nurses acknowledged her presence as she walked around. She had done well, he thought. What had he done? But he had now got the facts, or at least some of them, his father had been accepted into the college, he had held his nerve to win a fortune, and he now almost knew what he would do now. He now needed to get well and talk with his mother about what he now knew. But he did not know everything.

The days passed and he grew stronger. The worst of the malaria was over the new drugs had worked, he felt anew each day. Jim McCabe, as others left, stayed on to help in the hospital and soon had regular ward duties. He was good company and Marion liked him.

Gunter and Anya returned the following day, and the days after, filling in the details of how they identified the rising star and how it turned out that Pink Star won the day. They painted in the jigsaw of pieces about how the Bowery boys were overcome by Cana Gael and how the adventure began. Gunter was in his element as usual asking the first question. How did your father do it? We both became rich men that day. Enough for Cana Gael. Enough for us. Days passed and Owen's recovery continued until Marion announced he was to be discharged. Well enough to go home, well enough to go to Ireland. He knew now his mother was ill and could die. Arrangements made by Marion and Jim ensured a sea trip was the only viable option. Travelling by sea was still not easy. Most harbours were still on war alert. War time restrictions still applied and navigation was made more difficult with harbour lights extinguished and navigation buoys removed. And of course there was always the danger of the rogue sea mine. Tales abounded of near misses and those that had come to grief in stormy waters. Yet strangely Owen look forward to seeing the

Fastnet Rock, a small inlet in the Atlantic Ocean, the most southerly point in Ireland and the last sight his father would have seen of his home country, often called Ireland's teardrop. Within days Marion Jim and Owen were travelling overland to the Port of Montreal located on the East coast and the St Lawrence sea way offering the shortest distance to travel by sea to Europe. When they arrived, moored up on Wing No1 was a ship with Eire painted on its side, and the neutral flag of Ireland, the Irish tricolour painted below. Owen was aware that the neutral path De Valera had set, had caused increasing problems despite the war being over, of maintaining self -sufficiency especially in food and fuel, mainly as a consequence of having no navy to speak of. Owen and Jim began to cement their relationship again and Owen was glad when he offered to join the exodus to Ireland. Yet his relationship with Marion took a quieter path. Even though he'd been discharged he still wasn't his old self. Maybe he never would be. His body needed more time, despite Marion taking his temperature, his pulse and blood pressure each day. His mind needed even longer. Incarceration had left its scars. There was never the right moment; he struggled with not only where to start the conversation but also where it might head or even end. It was a strange time, the end of war and consequent lull in hostilities, created an insecure feeling that they should be doing something. And so it was the silence grew and sooner or later it would have to be broken. Soon the journey by ship was coming to an end, the Fastnet rock had been passed and Queenstown Harbour beckoned like two open arms ready to embrace its new returnees. Marion had already let Owens's mother and sister know when they hoped to arrive. As the ship pulled into its berthing place Owen could already see his sister standing on the harbour dock despite the fact she'd matured and changed into a shapely young woman he recognised her instantly. Even though they had not seen each other for such a long period of time, the first hug seemed to make time stand still. Owen introduced Jim but Marion needed no introduction. "As beautiful as ever," remarked Owen's sister, whereas Owen was greeted with, 'You've grown.' Owen laughed, and then they all laughed, ecstatic in their meeting. They held hands as they walked together.

Within the day , Owen was entering the door to Doyle's 's Farm. His mother lay sleeping, but a sixth sense, maybe the echo of a familiar voice, made her stir and a glint of light entered her part opened eyes. It was a moment of joy, frail as she was, she extended her arms towards him and embraced. Mother and son reunited. Owen felt the fragility in her body and that time was ebbing. He kissed her hands. Marion placed her hand on his shoulder. A sense of urgency overtook his mother," I need to tell you things. When I first saw your father, I knew in the moment in the ticket office, all that time ago, that here was a man I could love with all my heart."And then she blurted out with closed eyes.' I should never have stopped him becoming a priest'.

" 'It's alright I know what happened. He didn't wait for the college to offer him a place. When he was faced with taking the Cana Gael bounty back to Ireland instantly he made the choice. He chose you. He chose to keep us safe. In his heart he knew what he was giving up. He

212

loved you with all of his being . He chose the better life.."

As if feeling relieved , her eyes flickered unsteadily open for a few seconds and she said in a whispered voice.' Thank you. Marion knows what to do I sent her a package. She needs to take you somewhere." A slow smile temporarily brightened her face.

Marion, answered "Tomorrow."

His mother continued ," Joe was a misguided man , I made a mistake . I'm sorry if he hurt you. God knows he died a terrible death. Forgive me. she said punctuated with short breaths"

"There is nothing to forgive. Rest now we'll talk tomorrow." But it was not to be. This was the last conversation he would have with his mother.

She, Mary, died the following morning whilst the priest, Father Ryan was giving her absolution.

Despite the sorrow of death the following morning, Marion, who carried a package, took Owen for a walk. They walked along the wind- swept pathways brimming over with luxuriant sea pinks and blue cornflowers. Owen felt reborn. He stooped to pick flowers as he walked. "Do you remember what you gave me all those years ago when you left Ireland."

He nodded. She produced from her purse a small locket which when she opened it displayed a faded blue flower. He remembered well the kiss and how much it pained him to leave, But life had changed them. Had they grown apart? Was he still the same person? Was she still the same? But life had already changed them. Did they still have dreams and ambitions? "We were young then, we thought we were invincible. If only I had waited for Connor to find the walking stick I would never have joined the British army." As he said this Marion sat down on part of a low mossy wall enclosing a piece of green land . "What lovely views," as if ignoring his thoughts. Owen had to nod ,he could see for miles in all directions. In the centre there was the beginnings of some foundations of a derelict house. He stood still absorbing the moment. What a fabulous place to build a house he thought.

"Isn't it lovely I saw it when I was last in Ireland .Your mother was well enough, and took me to it and gave me this package. Which I now give to you." Owen took the parcel and inside found a set of Deeds in his name and some notes in his father's handwriting. He looked up and looked incredulously into Marion's eyes realising he owned this piece of land. It was his to build on. A little piece of Ireland, a green field . He read again,

'Remember I said I would find you the fifth green field, a place of sanctuary, live a good life.' Suddenly Owen felt uneasy thoughts creep through his head. He knew what he had to do. He looked at her with dark eyes heavy with fatigue. Heavy with sorrow over his mother's passing. But he had asked the questions a thousand times in his head. How is it possible to hold two opposing ideas in your mind but neither are attainable without intense colossal pain. Are there no ambitions noble enough to justify breaking someone's heart. He had this hour, this moment in which to tell Marion what was on his mind. All the time the thousands of questions haunted him, and yet he was driven by a fierce desire to say how much he loved her. He had just said goodbye to his mother, and Connor before, and a vision of Matt hung in his head and now he contemplated a further last goodbye. He had lived without her and yet he was consumed with her every waking moment. And yet now could now he consider the blackest of decisions. Part of him felt life had cheated them and led them apart from each other. What will he say ? She possible already knew the truth. She knew that his thoughts lingered on what his father wished for him, to join the priest hood and what that meant for their future together. In the end he pulled her close ," I need to find out if my father's wishes are my wishes," .he whispered in her ear in a halting voice. " so I need to tell you I have today already secured a place to become priest at Dunwoody Seminary beginning in a week's time" Marion drew a sharp, surprised breath. but she knew in her heart that he had found it painful. She struggled hard to hold back the tears. "I need to find out if it is my calling. Can we take it slowly. Can I ask will you wait for me."

"One year?"

"One year and I'll be back"

"No you go I'll be here when you get back"

He knew in his heart she may not. He knew he may not come back. But that was for another day , another life.

He, looked down at the flowers in his hands and knew he had made a promise to a dear friend He took her hand , and kept his promise.

Bibliography

I am grateful to the following authors for the secure factual information which support the history of key events and personalities that form the backdrop to this novel. This novel is also informed by stories and events that illuminated the lives of my Irish father and my Irish grandfather. The following books were invaluable:

1   Thomas Bartlett " Ireland- A History"

     ISBN 978-1-107-42234-6

2   Richard Killeen   "Ireland Land, people and History"

     ISBN 978-1-84901-439-7

3   Robert Widders "The Emperor's Irish Slaves"

     ISBN 978-1-84588-72-78

4   Eric Lomax   "The Railway Man

     ISBN 0-09-958-231-7

5   Google and Wikepedia

Acknowledgements

I am also indebted for the help and encouragement of my wife Paula, my son Steve and his wife Vicki, Kevin my brother, to Julia for proof reading and to Dereck for advice and support and everyone in the writing group for the gracious way they commented on my story.

Printed in Poland
by Amazon Fulfillment
Poland Sp. z o.o., Wrocław

61511078R00123